TEXAS RIDER

Center Point
Large Print

Also by Bradford Scott and available from
Center Point Large Print:

Gunsmoke on the Rio Grande
The Hate Trail
The Slick-Iron Trail

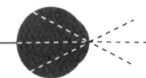

**This Large Print Book carries the
Seal of Approval of N.A.V.H.**

TEXAS RIDER

Bradford Scott

CENTER POINT LARGE PRINT
THORNDIKE, MAINE

This Center Point Large Print edition
is published in the year 2018 by arrangement with
Golden West Literary Agency.

The text of this Large Print edition is unabridged.
In other aspects, this book may vary
from the original edition.
Printed in the United States of America
on permanent paper.
Set in 16-point Times New Roman type.

ISBN: 978-1-68324-693-0 (hardcover)
ISBN: 978-1-68324-697-8 (paperback)

Library of Congress Cataloging-in-Publication Data

The Library of Congress has cataloged record
under LCCN: 2017052055

Printed and bound in Great Britain
by TJ International Ltd, Padstow, Cornwall

MIX
Paper from
responsible sources
FSC
www.fsc.org   FSC® C013056

ONE

East from Morton, in southwest Texas, a trail runs. It winds across the level rangeland, climbs the long slopes of a range of low hills and vanishes through a dark and narrow notch in the hill crests. Beyond the hills it flows onward toward the rising sun, over prairie and desert, through fertile valleys, over towering ridges to reach the far-off Nueces country and the valley of the Sabine, the watery bar to the eastern gate of Texas. It is a well-traveled trail, for it is the gateway to the Southwest. West of Morton it flows on and branches, one arm—still well traveled—reaching hungrily for the sunshine of Southern California, the other slithering furtively into the grim and desolate fastnesses of the Big Bend country.

Morning sunlight was flooding the hill crests, but the narrow notch was still thronged with shadows and ghostly wreaths of mist.

Suddenly, through the curtain of mist burst something that gleamed like a star in the gloom. It rolled forward, resolved into a great white object swaying and lurching. Eight plodding horses took form, dragging the huge vehicle by straining traces. Another star burned from the mist, and another, and another, until more than two score of the ponderous wains were rumbling down the trail to the level rangeland.

Covered wagons! The "ships of the prairie," the vanguard of empire, slow, methodical, resistless in their advance. The old trail had known them before, as had the trails to the north and the trails to the south. Gold hunter, adventurer, home seeker and Mormon had used them in their onward march to the blue waters of the Pacific. They were an old story, now. Time was when they startled the Indians of the plains and sent them flying to their fellows with tales of ghosts and demons riding the wings of the wind. Soon the Indians understood them, saw in them opportunities for loot. And also quickly understood them to be the symbol of a force that would in the end sweep the red man from the land. This was no longer a vision of the dim future, but an accomplished fact.

Beside the wagons rode men on horseback, rangy, gaunt men for the most part, with watchful eyes, ready rifles hooked under their arms. Their gaze was to the front, these lean soldiers of the sod, their eyes hopeful but shadowed by hardship and disappointment.

In the forefront rode a blocky, alert-looking young man—Van Worthington, the appointed leader of the train, whose word was law. The tall, amazingly gaunt, burning-eyed horseman at his side was the Reverend Elijah Crane, the pastor of the church to which the emigrants had belonged in far-off Kentucky. Elijah Crane's thin, thought-worn features and haggard cheeks bespoke one who had fought, and won, a sore fight against worldly passions and desires but had suffered greatly in the contest; who in crushing the inward foe, had come close to crushing himself. But from the burning eyes under the craggy, tufted brows flashed a fierce energy, the heritage of the fighting stock from which he was descended. With compressed lips and clouded brow, he sat his horse, stiffly upright, the very genius and personification of asceticism, and rife with the opinionated views and intolerance that too often go hand in hand with asceticism.

Cowhands and ranch owners sighted the wagon train as it rolled westward across the prairie, eyed it with decided disfavor and prepared to repel an unwelcome invasion. However, the train moved on across the lush rangeland, apparently headed for the cattle and mining town of Morton.

The sun was high in the sky when the train halted on a level spot on the banks of a stream about a mile east of Morton. The emigrants at once set about making camp. Van Worthington and Elijah Crane continued on to town.

An hour or so later, Sheriff John Stockley entered his office, his rugged face mirroring concern.

Seated comfortably in a tilted chair, the high

heels of his riding boots hooked over a rung, was Ranger Walt Slade, named by the Mexican *peones* of the Rio Grande river villages, *El Halcón*—the Hawk. He glanced expectantly at the sheriff, an old friend.

"It's a big one," Stockley said without preamble. "Better'n forty wagons. The feller in charge, name's Worthington, rode in and talked with me. Seemed to be a right hombre. Those folks are from Kentucky. They settled over in the Nueces country last year, but it was so hot and dry they couldn't do no good. They're farmers, you see. They decided to pull up stakes again and head west, looking for a place to settle; but so far they haven't had any luck. There's no place for them here, as you know, the way the cowmen of this section feel about nesters, as they call 'em. I hate to see folks up against it like that, but what in blazes can we do about them?"

Slade rolled a cigarette before replying. When the brain tablet was going to his satisfaction, he spoke.

"I think, John, that I'll ride with this one, if I can manage it."

The sheriff regarded him, his brow wrinkled. "Scairt the same thing might happen to this one as did to the other two that passed this way?" he asked.

"Not beyond the realm of possibility," Slade answered.

"It was an ugly business," growled the sheriff. "Wagons burned, all the men shot, and the women and kids packed off the devil knows where."

"To be sold as slaves to the outlaws and the tribes down in the Mexican mountains," Slade said. "A good market for white women and children in the Sinaloa hills."

"I wouldn't have believed there were still that many wild Indians running loose in Texas and organized into a raiding band," growled the sheriff.

"There are not," Slade said.

"Of course there's still plenty down in Mexico, in the Carmen Mountains country, for instance," continued the sheriff. "But I never heard of 'em raiding up here in force."

"And you never will," Slade stated positively. Sheriff Stockley snorted, and tugged his mustache.

"Folks say the hellion who leads the pack is old Bajo El Sol, the great war chief and Mexican raider. But as I understand it, Bajo El Sol was killed years ago."

"He was," Slade said.

"Even if he wasn't, he'd be an old man now," resumed the sheriff. "And the sidewinder they talk about sure isn't old. Big and tall, more'n six feet high, built and walks like a panther. Got flashing black eyes and black hair and is mean as

9

a striped snake. I gather that old Bajo was a tough and salty hombre but that there wasn't anything mean or cruel about him. He was just a fighting man who held his comb high."

Slade nodded agreement and gazed out the window. Sheriff Stockley regarded him curiously.

"What you thinking about, Walt?" he asked. "You look a million miles away."

"I was recalling a line from Swinburne's poem, 'The Garden of Proserpine'," Slade replied. "It goes: 'That dead men rise up never.' "

Sheriff Stockley looked puzzled.

"And?" he prompted.

"And, I was—wondering," Slade said.

The sheriff looked even more puzzled. "Now what the devil do you mean by that?" he complained.

Slade laughed. "Just thinking out loud," he parried.

"You ain't hintin' old Bajo's come back to life?" Stockley remarked suspiciously.

"Hardly," Slade smiled, and continued to gaze out the window.

The sheriff regarded him in silence. What a splendid-looking man he was, he thought. More than six feet tall, the breadth of his shoulders and the depth of his chest, slimming down to a sinewy waist, matched his height. His thick, crisp hair was so black a blue shadow seemed to lie upon it. The rather wide mouth, grin-quirked at the corners, relieved somewhat the touch of fierceness evinced in the prominent hawk nose above and the lean, powerful chin and jaw beneath.

It was the eyes, however, that held the sheriff's attention. Pale gray eyes fringed by long black lashes, they were cold eyes that nevertheless always seemed to have little devils of laughter dancing in their clear depths. At times those gay, reckless devils would leap to the fore, their hands full of sunshine. At other times, the sheriff knew, they could be grim and terrible as the pale shadow of Death's approaching wing.

Slade wore the homely, efficient garb of the rangeland with careless grace—soft blue shirt, Levi's, well-scuffed half boots of softly tanned leather, somewhat battered, broad-brimmed "J.B.," vivid handkerchief looped about his sinewy throat. Around his lean waist were double cartridge belts, from the carefully worked and oiled cutout holsters of which protruded the black butts of heavy guns. And from these long guns his slender, powerful hands seemed never far away.

All in all, he looked the part of a chuck-line riding cowhand who gave rather more than average thought to his personal appearance; which was just how he wished to appear.

Abruptly, he turned from the window. "John," he said, "suppose we ride out and pay those folks a visit. Perhaps I can manage to persuade them to let me ride with them."

"Okay," nodded the sheriff, adding with a grin, "but if they learn about you, maybe they won't want the notorious El Halcón tagging along with 'em."

"We'll have to chance that," Slade smiled.

" 'The singingest man in the whole Southwest, with the fastest gunhand,' " the sheriff quoted, the grin broadening.

"Somewhat of an exaggeration on both counts," Slade replied.

To that, the peace officer's only reply was a derisive snort.

Just the same, there was something to what the sheriff had previously said. Because of his habit of working undercover whenever possible and often not revealing his Ranger connections, Walt Slade had built up a remarkable dual reputation. To those who knew the truth, he was regarded as not only the most fearless but also the ablest of the illustrious body of law enforcement officers. Others, who knew him only as El Halcón, of dubious reputation with killings to his credit, were wont to declare vigorously that he was just a blasted outlaw too smart to get caught though he would get his come-uppance sooner or later.

Slade did nothing to discourage this erroneous conception although, as Captain Jim McNelty, the famous Commander of the Border Battalion of the Texas Rangers, often pointed out, it laid him open to serious personal danger at the hands of some trigger-happy marshal or deputy or gun slinger out to get a reputation by downing El Halcón. For he knew being known as El Halcón opened avenues of information that would be closed to a Ranger. So despite Captain Jim's grumbling and dire predictions, as El Halcón went on his carefree way, satisfied with the present and confident the future would take care of itself.

"Come on," said the sheriff. "Let's get our cayuses and hightail."

Together they rode out of town, the sheriff forking a rangy roan, Slade riding Shadow, his tall black, declared by many to be the finest horse in Texas and as well known in various quarters as his master.

And as they rode, from the depths of a murky saloon, a two-legged coyote watched them go. After making sure they were headed for the farmers' encampment, he hurried to another and larger coyote who was close to the big he-wolf of the pack, as close as that sinister individual ever allowed anybody to get to him.

"Wherever that blankety-blank El Halcón shows up there's trouble," growled coyote Number Two. "I betcha he's cooking up some scheme to get in with the nesters and work things to feather his own nest. You sift sand to the Boss and let him know. And," he added reflectively, "maybe I can do a little chore on the hellion."

"Better be careful," advised coyote Number One. "Monkeying with El Halcón is a good way to bust up a dull day for the undertaker."

"He's salty, all right, but I've a notion he's a mite exaggerated," grunted coyote Number Two. "Find Pete and Moore and send them here. Then get going to the Boss. Maybe I'll have some good news for him in the morning."

Left alone, coyote Number Two leaned back in his chair and rolled a cigarette, his hard-lined face wearing a smug expression.

TWO

When Slade and Stockley reached the camp and dismounted, Van Worthington and Elijah Crane strode forward to greet them. Stockley performed the introductions. Worthington shook hands, with a firm grip, but Crane merely ducked his head and did not extend his hand, an omission that caused the corners of Slade's mouth to quirk a little.

"Folks who know him sorta have a habit of coming to Walt when they need advice or a helping hand," the sheriff explained. "He's young but he's got plenty of wrinkles on his horns. Uh-huh, he's right there with the savvy and I've

14

a notion he might be able to give you folks a lift, somehow or other."

"We need one," Worthington replied. "All we ask is a place to settle down, build homes and grow crops. We're willing to work hard and put up with plenty if we can just get a chance to do for ourselves. We're hunting for a place we were told about. Last year Silas Austin, one of our folks, was over here to the west looking around for a place that might do. Somewhere to the west of here, in the country I believe folks call the Big Bend, he hit on a place he thought all right. A sort of hidden valley walled around by hills and mighty rough country. He said some Mexican fellers told him about it; they had a funny name for it, 'Valley of Lost Stars'." Walt Slade suddenly looked interested.

"Yes, Valley of Lost Stars," Worthington repeated. "They said a long, long time back a lot of stars fell there and were never seen any more. They told Si how to get there. He said it was just what they said it was. That the grass was poor because it was all brush grown and he reckoned that's why the cattle-raising fellers never claimed it. But he said the soil was good and rich and could be cleared and would grow fine crops once it was cleared. Sounded good to us, so we decided to make a try for it. But after we'd sold out what we had in the Nueces country—for mighty little, I might add—and were getting ready to start, Si all of a sudden took sick and died. He'd told us the general direction to the place but that's about all. We'd figured for him to guide us there. But, things being like they were, we decided we'd better make a try at finding the place, hoping that maybe we'd meet somebody who could direct us there. So far we ain't had any luck."

"Valley of Lost Stars," Slade repeated. "I think I've heard of the place. Has another name, I believe: *Espantosa*—Haunted Valley."

"Why, that's right!" exclaimed Worthington, his face brightening. "Si mentioned that. He said the Mexican fellers wouldn't go near the place—they believed it was haunted, and they told him the Indians never would either. Yes, it must be the same place. And do you know how to get there, Mr. Slade?"

"Yes, I think I do," El Halcón replied. "It's a rough road and a dangerous road, but I've a notion I could find the place. If I'm right, and I believe I am, there's a passable way to the railroad town fifty-some miles to the north. Incidentally, what did your friend say about water? The Bend is a dry country and you can't do much without water."

"He said there was plenty," Worthington instantly replied. "Said there were plenty of trees, too, plenty for building."

"Sounds good, Walt," interpolated the sheriff.

"Yes, it does," Slade agreed. "I'd say it's about

two hundred miles from here, by the way the wagons would have to go, but no reason why a train can't get through."

"And you'll tell us how to get there, Mr. Slade?" Worthington asked eagerly.

"Mr. Worthington, if you won't think I am presuming, I believe I can do better than that," Slade replied. "I've been getting itchy feet of late and have to move on. Seeing as I'd planned to trail my twine in that general direction, I see no reason why I can't guide you to your valley, being reasonably sure as to about where it is located."

The young man stared at him, and his eyes were moist, his voice unsteady as he replied.

"Why—why, Mr. Slade, that—that is mighty fine of you," he faltered. "It's wonderful! What do you think, Reverend Crane?"

Elijah Crane had all the while been regarding Slade with scant favor.

"I am not so sure," he rumbled. "Indeed, I think it is a questionable step. This young man strikes me as being one of the ungodly. We do not even know if he is of our Faith."

Sheriff Stockley bristled. "Why, you ungrateful old horned toad!" he began, but Slade quelled him with a gesture. And the devils of laughter in his eyes had abruptly jumped to the front.

"Take it easy, John," he counseled. "I've a notion the Reverend and I will make out together before all's said and done."

Van Worthington turned to Elijah Crane. His face was stern.

"Reverend," he said, "you are the shepherd of your flock but I am in charge of this train, and what I say goes. We'll accept the offer gladly. Mr. Slade, I apologize for the Reverend's rudeness and I hope it will not cause you to withdraw your generous offer."

"Offer still stands," Slade replied cheerfully. Worthington again thrust out his hand. Elijah Crane regarded them from under his shaggy brows.

" 'He who sups with Satan needs a long-handled spoon,' " he observed sententiously, and walked away. The devils of laughter appeared, to turn gleeful somersaults before retiring to their accustomed habitat in the back of Slade's eyes.

"There is one condition attached to my offer, Mr. Worthington," Slade said. "Shortly after leaving here, we will be traversing dangerous country. Country with which I am acquainted and with which you are not. I shall expect any order I give to be obeyed implicitly, at once, and without question. The lives of all of us may well depend on such obedience."

"Guess I'd be a damn fool to argue that point," Worthington said bluntly. "I'll follow your lead, and so will everybody else, including the Reverend, despite his grumbling and grouching."

"That'll be fine," Slade said. For a moment he

studied the young man's face, lined beyond its years, slightly haggard.

"Mr. Worthington," he said, "I think you've been pushing yourself a mite too hard of late. Suppose you drop in at the sheriff's office after dark and you and I will mosey around a bit and sort of relax. Okay?"

"I'll be glad to," Worthington accepted gratefully. "I do feel a mite worn."

"Okay," Slade repeated. "Be seeing you. Come on, John, let's head for town."

There was a pleased expression in El Halcón's eyes as they mounted and headed for Morton, but Sheriff Stockley was in anything but a good temper.

"That dadgummed old coot! I shoulda busted him one!" he declared wrathfully.

Slade reached over and laid a soothing hand on his angry friend's arm.

"We who are tolerant must practice tolerance even toward the intolerant," he said. "Arrogant, narrow, opinionated; but, I'll wager, a strong stick to lean on in time of trouble."

The sheriff snorted, and looked decidedly unconvinced, but did not discuss Crane further.

"Young Worthington seems all right, though," he remarked a little later. "He told me he lost his wife about a year back; has a little boy just six years old."

"A grave responsibility," Slade commented.

"And he strikes me as a man who takes his responsibilities very seriously. The care of the train weighs heavily on him."

"He sure was grateful to you," said the sheriff.

"And it made me feel a trifle hypocritical," Slade replied. "After all, I was very anxious to accompany the train."

"Because it's part of your work and the reason for you being here," the sheriff pointed out.

"Yes," Slade conceded. "Something has got to be done about the raids on wagon trains. More and more of them are coming, and they must be protected from the vultures of organized crime."

"Doesn't look like any Indian band would tackle a train the size of this one," observed Stockley.

"No Indian band would," Slade answered. The sheriff shot him a curious glance.

"And you still don't believe a roving band from one of the reservations is responsible?"

"I certainly do not," Slade replied. "That's the impression being given, of course. And a few sheriffs and marshals are busy chasing after Indians that don't exist."

"Including me," grinned Stockley, who had a sense of humor. "But everybody who's got a look at them swears they're black Apaches."

"All and sundry don't get a look at raiding Indians," Slade pointed out. "If you get a look at them, the chances are it'll be the last look you get

20

at anything. In this particular instance, scrub off the dye and you'll find white skins beneath it."

"Walt, do you really mean that?" Stockley asked incredulously.

"I do," Slade replied.

"Oh, well," the sheriff sighed. "You always seem to be right, so I reckon I'll have to string along with you. Anyhow, it'll save me saddle sores—chasing after Indians that don't exist."

"And while you're at it, you might keep a close eye on things right here in Morton," Slade advised. "I've a notion some of the hellions show up here every now and then, and no doubt in Marathon, over to the west."

"We get all sorts in this blasted pueblo, what with the spreads and the mines and the two trails crossing," growled the sheriff. "That's why I've got a branch office here, as you know. Well, here we are; let's put up our broncs and then go get something to eat."

Shortly after dark, Van Worthington put in an appearance at the sheriff's office, where Slade awaited him. He was dressed much the same as the Ranger, only his riding boots had flat heels and his broad-brimmed hat was black. On his hip he packed an old long-barreled Smith & Wesson Forty-four. He grinned a trifle sheepishly as he noted the direction of Slade's gaze.

"Seems everybody around here wears one, and

I didn't want to look conspicuous," he explained. "I can't pull and shoot like you Texas fellers, but I do hit what I aim at."

"Which is the important thing," Slade said. "I've known quite a few quick-draw gun slingers to get their come-uppance from gents who weren't overly fast but who put the first shot where it counted. Well, suppose we amble over to the Alhambra across the street first and have a drink just to get the feel of things."

"What a pair!" snorted the sheriff. "Well, I'll come and pick up the bodies."

"We're plumb peaceful," Slade declared.

"Uh-huh, so is a stick of dynamite till somebody sets it off," grunted the sheriff. "Be seeing you."

THREE

Although it was still early, Morton was beginning to hum. Cow ponies stood at the long hitchracks and their riders were already crowding the bars, of which Morton boasted plenty. A gabble of conversation and strains of music came over the swinging doors, sometimes with song or what was apparently intended for it. Slade was pleased to see that his companion's eyes were brightening and that the lines in his face seemed to be smoothing out somewhat. He felt that a

22

mite of diversion with bright lights and hilarity were just what the young farmer needed.

"A good night to see the town," he remarked. "Payday for the spreads hereabouts and that always makes things lively."

"Guess I can stand a mite of liveliness," Worthington replied. "I sure haven't seen much of it during the past few months. Reckon the Reverend would call this a sink of iniquity," he added with a chuckle. "But I don't pay him much mind."

"The Reverend might not be too far off, according to his standards," Slade smiled. "These cow and mining towns aren't exactly a Sunday school picnic on payday nights."

They had a drink in the Alhambra and then strolled about the town, pausing now and then for another snort. Worthington conversed animatedly, but Slade, whose eyes were everywhere, was mostly silent and very much on the alert. For it hadn't taken him long to spot the three men who were unobtrusively trailing them, and he felt pretty sure they were not motivated by idle curiosity. It looked like his El Halcón reputation had gotten around.

Gradually they worked their way toward the quieter portion of the town. Across the street was a row of warehouses, their darkened windows providing good imitations of mirrors, and by the reflections Slade was able to keep a close watch on the sinister trio without turning his head. He saw that they were gradually closing the distance.

"Let's drop in here," he suggested as they approached a rather dingy-looking saloon that appeared not too well lighted.

As they entered, he saw that the ceiling was low and supported by a couple of rows of stout posts. The bar was directly across from the entrance and the door was reflected in the back bar mirror; which was all to the good.

They reached the bar and he was just about to tell Worthington, "Keep behind me," when the farmer spoke up, his eyes on the dance floor.

"Wonder if one of those girls over there would dance with me?" he asked. "I like to dance."

"Of course, that's what they're here for; go ahead and ask one," Slade replied, glad to get his companion away from his side for the moment.

Worthington headed for the dance floor. Slade stood at the bar, watching the door in the mirror. He saw the three men enter, spreading out along the wall, and knew exactly what that meant. As their hands dropped to their holsters he whirled, drew and shot with both Colts, again and again. The room rocked with the bellow of gunfire.

One of the gunmen pitched forward on his face. Slade reeled slightly as a slug grazed the top of his shoulder. A second man fell with a gurgling scream, blood gushing from his bullet-slashed throat.

The third man ducked behind a post and pulled trigger. About all Slade could see of him was a slice of face and his leveled gun barrel.

From the dance floor boomed a shot. The slice of face was suddenly a mask of blood and shredded flesh as the man staggered back and fell, to lie motionless.

Slade, thumbs hooked over the cocked hammers of his guns, swept the room with his eyes. Under that icy gaze, the rising tumult abruptly stilled and men stood rigid. Satisfied that there was no hostile intent on the part of the crowd, he holstered his guns as Worthington came striding from the dance floor, the old Smith in his hand.

"Told you I hit what I aim at," he remarked. "And old Betsy here plugs right where she's held."

"And quite likely saved me from getting plugged," Slade replied. "The sidewinder was pretty well shielded by that post. Thanks."

"Glad to be of service," Worthington said cheerfully. "But how in tarnation did you do it? I was looking at you when the row started and those guns just seemed to grow in your hands, and you didn't seem to take aim at all."

"Practice, mostly," Slade answered. "Perhaps I'll be able to teach you the hang of it.

"And how about serving us a drink?" he suggested to the wide-eyed, open-mouthed bartender.

"Y-yes, sir! Y-es, sir! Coming right up, sir!"

quavered that worthy, who was shivering like a dog sitting on cactus spines.

"And you might notify the sheriff of what happened if he didn't hear the shooting, unless he is on his way here already," Slade added.

"Yes, sir, right away, sir," the drink juggler replied and beckoned a swamper.

The room was again in an uproar. "Blazes! did you ever see such shootin'!" a voice cried. "Who the devil is *he?*"

"Don't you know?" another voice bawled. "That's El Halcón, the outlaw!"

Jim Worthington shot his companion a startled glance. Then he turned in the direction of the voice.

"If I can find the skunk who said that," he announced clearly, "I'll put an air hole in his hide."

Nobody appeared to crave the distinction. Worthington turned back to Slade, raised his glass and took a sip.

"Here's to straight shooting," he said, and drained the glass with evident relish. Slade chuckled. He had a feeling that young Jim Worthington was a man to ride the river with.

"I'm getting gladder and gladder you consented to guide us to the Valley of Lost Stars," Worthington announced as he hammered on the bar for a refill.

"But how about the Reverend?" Slade smiled.

"Oh, don't worry about the Reverend," Worthington returned. "He's got you tagged as a brand to be snatched from the burning, and he's always hankering for a chance to do some snatching. Wonder why those skunks tried to kill you?"

"Well, you heard what somebody called me," Slade replied. "El Halcón is not very well liked in certain quarters."

"Guess it's to your credit if that sort doesn't like you," Worthington declared stoutly.

"Suppose we go see what we bagged," Slade suggested.

They pushed their way through the crowd gathered about the bodies, men respectfully making way for them. The three would-be killers were hard-bitten appearing characters with nothing outstanding about them so far as Slade could ascertain.

"Typical Border scum, the sort that would down their own mothers if the price were right," he remarked.

"Feller, I know that little one," somebody said. "He was called Apache Pete. He's got Indian blood."

"Ain't got as much as he had a while back," somebody else remarked. "Slug ripped his neck wide open. Here comes the sheriff!"

"Hope he doesn't throw me in jail," Worthington whispered apprehensively.

"More likely he'll pin a medal on you," Slade reassured him.

Sheriff Stockley nodded to Slade and Worthington, glanced at the bodies.

"*They* look plumb peaceable," he remarked pointedly.

Somewhat to Slade's surprise, men instantly crowded around the sheriff.

"We saw it all, John," they chorused. "Those hellions came in looking for trouble and got just what was coming to them. They throwed down on El Halcón soon as they got inside the door. He did for two of 'em and this farmer feller plugged the other one that was hiding behind a post. It was plain self-defense and we'll swear to it."

"All right, all right," said the sheriff. "You can swear to it at the inquest tomorrow. Come on, Slade, and you, too, Worthington, let's have a drink. Guess you'd better stick around tomorrow, Worthington, for the inquest. Won't hurt your critters to have a day of rest."

"Yes, they can stand a day or two of rest, if folks here don't mind," said Worthington.

"Nobody's going to begrudge you all the grass and water and rest you want," replied the sheriff. "Not all cowmen have horns, any more than all farmers have tails and cloven hoofs. Besides, it's all owned land hereabouts—no open range to kick up a ruckus over. Stick around for as long as you want to, and if you need a hand with something, just let me know."

"That's right," agreed the crowd. "You did a good chore, feller."

"You say one of 'em is Apache Pete?" remarked the sheriff. "I've had my eye on that horned toad for quite a while. Don't recognize the other two, but reckon they wear the same brand. Good riddance."

Heads nodded in agreement. The crowd drifted back to the bar, the dance floor and the games.

"My swampers will pack the carcasses to your office if you want 'em there, Sheriff," the saloon owner volunteered. The offer was accepted.

"Go through their pockets and let me know what you find," Slade said to Stockley, in low tones. "Might unearth something that will tie them up to somebody. I'll see you in the office later."

The sheriff nodded and raised his glass.

"Think I'll have another dance with that girl," announced Worthington. "That is if she ain't scared of me now."

"Try scaring a dance-floor gal!" snorted the sheriff. "Go to it."

Worthington ambled off; the sheriff turned to Slade.

"There's a table over in the corner where we can talk; suppose we squat there," he suggested.

"I'd like to hear the real lowdown on what happened."

After a waiter had taken their order, Stockley glanced inquiringly at Slade.

"Just a definite corroboration of my opinion as to what is going on," Slade said.

"Yes?" the sheriff prompted.

"Yes," Slade said. "Evidently the bunch learned I intended to ride with the wagon train and tried to stop me before I got started. And it brings me to the quote from Swinburne's poem."

"Believe I remember it.—'That dead men rise up never'?" the sheriff said. "What do you mean?"

"I mean," Slade said, "that a man I had all reason to believe dead is very much alive. There is a peculiarity about outlaws that never seems to fail. Their operations almost always fall into a definite pattern. Similar ways of doing things no matter where they're working. Similar objectives. The raids on the wagon trains are markedly similar to operations conducted up in the Panhandle by Veck Sosna, leader of the Comancheros, as ornery a bunch as ever forked a saddle. They also dealt in white women captives, selling them to the outlaws in the New Mexico hills and to the few Indian outfits still extant over there. Mostly young girls kidnapped from Mexico."

"Real hyderphobia skunks," growled the sheriff.

"You can say that double," Slade agreed. "And the man of whom I'm speaking was the worst of the lot, a regular devil. I succeeded in breaking up his gang, trailed him to his hidden hangout in the Cap Rock and thought I had him in my loop. But before I could catch up with him in a race across the prairie, he grabbed a freight train and got away clean."

"And that was the last you heard of him till now?" Slade shook his head.

"No," he replied. "For nearly two years, off and on between other chores, I trailed him. Finally caught up with him down around Boquillas, Mexico, where he was posing as a crippled rancher and doing such a good job of it he fooled everybody, including myself, for quite a while. Dyed his black hair yellow, pretended to be near-sighted and wore thick-lensed, tinted glasses to hide his flashing black eyes, walked with a stoop to lessen his height, using a cane. Finally I caught on and managed to pretty well smash the outfit he'd gotten together down there, and Sosna and I had another showdown, or what I figured at the time to be a showdown."

Slade paused to roll and light a cigarette. Sheriff Stockley waited, his face mirroring deep interest.

"There is the cable of an overhead conveyor system—I helped install the darn thing—which is used by the Puerto Rico mining company to transport ore from Boquillas, Mexico, to Boquillas, Texas, on the north side of the river. I chased Sosna north to the Rio Grande. He had a good horse, almost as good as Shadow, but not quite. I was closing in on him when he reached the river bank. The Rio Grande was in flood and impossible to ford. I thought I had him. But he went up the south conveyor tower like a squirrel, grabbed hold of the cable and started hand over hand across the river. I followed and was gaining on him. Seeing that I would catch him before he got in the clear on the north side of the river, he stopped, and, hanging onto the darn cable, he shot it out with me. I think I got him in the arm. Anyhow, he lost his hold and went into the river and the current swept him into Boquillas Canyon. Everybody said it would be impossible for anybody to live through the canyon with the river in high flood, especially a wounded man. I was of that opinion, too, although I never was sure. Now I'm beginning to wonder if there really is such a thing as a charmed life. Time after time, Sosna escaped death by a seeming miracle."

"And you believe the hellion who heads the raiding outfit is Sosna?" asked the sheriff.

"I am convinced he is," Slade replied. "The description of the leader some folks say is old Bajo El Sol come back to life tallies perfectly with Sosna's description. And, as I said, the methods employed by this bunch are strikingly similar to Sosna's mode of operation. The attempt on my life tonight was a fair sample. I don't think Sosna engineered that one, though. He tried that method a couple of times and learned it wouldn't work. When he makes a try it will be in a more subtle fashion, and therefore more dangerous. Well, this will make my third try at corraling him; perhaps it'll prove to be the charm."

"The whole darn thing sounds like a yarn from a story book," the sheriff declared.

"Yes," Slade conceded, "from a book by a highly imaginative author. But Veck Sosna is no figment of the imagination; he's uncomfortably real."

"Well, I wouldn't want to be taking the trip you plan," said the sheriff. "Looks like you'll have a good man along with you in young Worthington. But I'm not so sure about that darned old preacher. He strikes me as being a cantankerous and contrary coot it'll be hard to get along with."

"A 'starn and jealous man, braw and sonsy,' as the Scotch would say," Slade smiled. "But I'll warrant he's at his best with his back to the wall; I'm not worried about him."

Once again Sheriff Stockley did not look convinced.

"I'll send for the coroner first thing in the morning," he said. "No sense in it, but he'll want to set on those carcasses. Reckon he figures he has to do something to earn his pay."

"No hurry," Slade replied. "Day after tomorrow will do just as well. Those wagon horses need a couple of days rest."

"Okay," nodded the sheriff. "We'll handle it that way, then."

"And it will give me a chance to get acquainted with some of the farmers," Slade added. "I'd like to know a little more about whom I have to deal with."

Worthington came over from the dance floor a little later and was informed of the decision.

"Suits me fine," he said. "I'd like to dance a few more numbers with that girl tomorrow night; I like her."

"She looks okay to me," Slade said.

"The girls here are," interpolated the sheriff. "Old Carson, the owner, won't have any other kind. His place may look a mite run down, but everything here is on the up and up. He says he figures it's better to pay his help well and have the right sort than to waste the money on fancy fixin's. Guess he's got the right notion."

"He has," Slade agreed.

"Guess I'd better be getting back to the camp, and see how everything's going," Worthington decided. "See you tomorrow, Walt, and you, too, Sheriff."

Worthington left, with a wave of his hand to the dance-floor girl, who looked pleased and waved back.

"Yes, he's all right," Slade said, with a look at Worthington's departing back.

"Now suppose we amble over to your office and have a look at what those three hellions may have on them."

The bodies revealed nothing of significance until Slade drew from Apache Pete's pocket a gold watch with a fob attached. On the fob was a gold seal depicting a bird hovering protectingly over a nest of young. Inscribed on an inner circle were the words, Union Justice & Confidence. On an outer circle, STATE OF LOUISIANA.

"Guess this corroborates my contention," Slade observed, passing it to the sheriff. "The Louisiana State Seal. And you'll recall that the second wagon train dry-gulched and destroyed was from Louisiana. This is part of the loot."

"By gosh, you're right!" exclaimed the sheriff. "And this little snake was one of the bunch!"

"Undoubtedly," Slade nodded.

"Well, as I said before, you never seem to be wrong," said Stockley. "This tightens the loop, all right. Now all you have to do is grab the hellions."

"Yes, that's all," Slade conceded dryly. "You can put that watch in the county treasury, along with the money you took off these devils. And now I'm going to bed."

FOUR

The following day, Slade met a number of the farmers and liked them. Not all were old. There were a number of young husbands and several unattached young males who appeared to regard the whole business as a good deal of a lark, as is the way with youth in any age or any clime. The women ranged from elderly and motherly to quite a few who were young and pretty. There were also quite a few children, who were typical of kids the world over.

All in all, a fine bunch of people, Slade thought, and he was glad of the chance to lend a helping hand.

"They're what Texas needs," he told Sheriff Stockley. "Folks of the right sort, who will build homes and change the wastelands into garden spots. Texas needs them to develop the good here that is enough and more for all."

"I think you're right," agreed the sheriff.

The inquest, held a day later, was brief, the verdict to the point and typical cow country; 'lowing that the three skunks got what was coming to them and commending Slade and Worthington for doing a good chore.

"Might as well have saved the jury fees," grumbled Stockley. "Everybody knew what the verdict was going to be. Oh, well, I got enough dinero from the pockets of those hellions to more than pay 'em."

On the fourth day of its arrival, Slade and Worthington sat their horses and watched the wagon train roll past, headed west. The young farmer's eyes were bright, his face ashine with pleasant memories.

"After we get settled, I'm coming back for that dance-floor girl," he announced. "She promised she'd wait and would be glad to go with me. And I'm sure glad we laid over here. Living alone and caring for a youngster ain't easy."

Slade smiled, his eyes sunny. He felt it was a good omen.

"What the devil!" he exclaimed abruptly.

The last huge wain was lurching past, and it was driven by a girl—a rather small girl with an unruly mop of curly brown hair cut short, very big and very blue eyes, and a mutinous red mouth.

Slade opened his lips to speak, and at that instant the off lead horse shied violently, slamming into his fellow and nearly knocking him off his feet. Slade's hand flashed down and up. Smoke spurted from the muzzle of his long Colt and the poised head of the coiled rattlesnake that had slithered onto the trail vanished. The writhing body slapped against the lead horse's foreleg and drove him frantic with fear. He reared high. The rest of the team swerved, the front wheels of the wagon locked, and the vehicle was in imminent danger of being overturned.

Slade sent Shadow surging forward. He left the saddle with the tall black still in motion, reached up and gripped the rearing horse's bit iron. Great muscles on arm and shoulder stood out plain under his thin shirt as he slammed the animal's front hoofs down onto the trail. The crazed horse tried to rear again, but Slade's iron strength held him helpless. Within a few seconds Slade had the team under control.

"Holy Pete!" exclaimed Worthington. "I wouldn't have believed there was a man alive who could do that."

"Good deal of a trick to it," Slade deprecated the feat.

"Uh-huh," Worthington agreed dryly. "About the same sort of trick as turning a mountain over with a toothpick."

"Who is the girl, and why is she driving?" Slade asked.

"She's Leela Austin, Si Austin's daughter," Worthington replied. "You'll rec'lect me telling you Si died just when we were getting ready to start from Kentucky. She insisted on coming along, alone. Don't hanker for company."

"Alone?" Slade repeated. "Nobody else in that wagon?"

"That's right," Worthington answered.

Slade loosed the quieted horse's bit and walked back to the wagon, Worthington pacing his mount beside him.

"This wagon doesn't bring up the rear," the Ranger announced. The girl stared at him, her round little white chin going up.

"I prefer to bring up the rear," she said crisply.

"Perhaps," Slade said, "but I prefer you don't." He whistled Shadow, mounted and rode ahead, pausing to speak to the drivers of the next three wagons, who obediently pulled aside. Slade turned his mount and rode back to the rear wagon.

"All right, Miss Austin, close up the gap," he directed. "That's your position in the train from now on."

The blue eyes, hot with anger, met the cold gray for a moment. Then, her lips compressed, her head high, she spoke to her horses and swept past him without a glance. Slade waited until her vehicle was in position, motioned to the other drivers, and reined in alongside Worthington,

"Well," the farmer said, "that makes twice today I've seen something I wouldn't have believed possible—the way you handled that horse and made Leela Austin do something she didn't want to do. I guess Si sorta spoiled her after her mother died, when she was just a tad. She's all right, but mighty uppity; she don't even take much from the Reverend. Why did you send her on ahead?"

"The rear of a wagon train is a danger point in hostile country," Slade explained. "Easy to cut out during a ruckus. Now, you see, I've got three wagons to the rear and each with two men on the driver's seat. Get the notion?"

"Guess I do," admitted Worthington.

"Well, everything appears to be lined up now," Slade said. "Come on, and we'll get in front of the column; that's our post from now on. After a bit I'll assign the horsemen to outriding whenever possible. That is, away from the trail on either side, so they can keep a watch on things."

"You figure we might have trouble?" Worthington asked curiously.

"Other trains have had trouble, and it is best to be prepared against a similar contingency," Slade replied. "Let's go."

All day the train rolled ahead slowly but steadily. Toward evening the horses were toiling up a long ridge. Slade and Worthington and Elijah Crane, who had joined them, riding ahead, reached the broad crest first. The stupendous panorama of the Big Bend lay before them, beautiful with a wild and lonely beauty, hideous with its gleaming deserts and naked rock. Gazing over the vast sweep of country, Van Worthington remarked wistfully, "There ought to be some place for us in all this."

" 'Foxes have holes, and birds of the air have nests,' " Slade quoted softly.

Elijah Crane instantly completed the quotation, " 'But the Son of man hath not where to lay his head!' "

Slade let the full force of his steady gray eyes rest on the stern old fanatic's face.

"Yes," he said, his deep voice all music. "But He also said, 'If then God so clothe the grass, which is today in the field, and tomorrow is cast into the oven, shall He not much more clothe you, O ye of little faith?' "

For a moment Elijah Crane stared at the tall Ranger. Then he rubbed his long blue chin and, saying nothing, turned his horse and rode back to meet the lead wagon, which was just topping the rise. Van Worthington gazed after him and chuckled.

"Guess you sorta hipped the Reverend," he said. "Calc'late he didn't expect to find you so well grounded in the Scriptures."

"The Bible and the Talmud, aside from their religious significance, are, I think, the grandest pieces of literature ever compiled," Slade replied. "They have always fascinated me, and it is not hard to remember quotable passages."

"You're a puzzler," Worthington complained querulously. "Half the time I don't know what

41

the devil you're saying. You dress like a cattle feller, but you sure don't talk like one."

"Not all cowhands are illiterate," Slade reminded him.

"Maybe not," Worthington conceded, "but I don't think many of them talk like a dictionary. I'd just about be willing to bet that maybe you went to college."

Slade smiled, and did not reply.

Van Worthington's guess was shrewd. Shortly before the death of his father, subsequent to financial reverses which entailed the loss of the elder Slade's ranch, young Walt had graduated from a famous college of engineering. He had planned to take a post-graduate course in special subjects to round out his education before settling down to the profession he had and still intended would be his life's work. That seeming out of the question for the time being, he lent a receptive ear when Captain Jim McNelty, with whom he had worked some during summer vacations, suggested that he join the Rangers for a while and continue his studies in spare time.

Long since, he had gotten more from private study than he could have hoped to obtain from the postgrad and was well fitted for a career of engineering. However, in the meantime Ranger work had gotten a strong hold on him, and he was loath to sever connections with the illustrious body of law enforcement officers. Plenty of time to be an engineer—he was young—he'd stick with the Rangers for a while.

Slade glanced over the ridge crest, which was really almost the width of a mesa, grass grown and with a small stream birthing in a spring which bubbled up in the shade of some trees.

"I think we might as well make camp for the night here," he said. "Not far beyond the foot of the ridge the trail forks. We take the south fork and it'll be rougher going than what you've yet experienced, with no good camping sites for quite some distance. We'll do better to spend the night here and hit the harder going in the morning."

He did not mention to his companion that the ridge crest was also favorable for keeping an eye on the surrounding terrain. He hardly expected trouble of any sort so near Morton, but it was wise to be cautious, conditions being what they were in the section.

"Okay," Worthington agreed. "I'll give the orders." He rode back to meet the advancing train.

For a while Slade sat his horse on the edge of the ridge, gazing out over the wild land beyond. Down there was the dark empire of outlawry, its mountains and valleys sanctuary for hunted men, where eternal vigilance was the price of safety. A land of blood and tears, where the struggle for existence was still primal.

And yet, it was a bountiful and virgin land, a

goal for the home hunter to strive for. Here the tide of Spanish invasion had split as on a mighty rock, flowing northward on the east and west of the great bow of the Rio Grande, in the vast curve of which lay the Texas Big Bend, making scant impress on the land which was the Bend. Here cattle required wide acreage; but the needle and wheat grasses and the succulent curly mesquite would plump out a gaunt old steer in no time.

Here the plow was still almost unknown; but the soil was rich and just awaiting the sower's hand to yield a bountiful harvest. All in all, despite its difficulties and hazards, it was a good land, Slade thought, and he welcomed the chance to lead courageous souls to it. Savage men and a savage terrain might strive to balk them, but he was confident that neither would succeed. And he was also confident that here in the rugged wastelands would be written the final chapter of the saga of El Halcón versus Veck Sosna, the Panhandle outlaw. Who would ride away after the showdown? Slade shrugged his broad shoulders and gave that little thought.

He was aroused from his reverie by the voice of Van Worthington.

"Come on and eat," the farmer called. "I eat with the Cranes," he said when Slade joined him. "They sort of look after me. Look after little Tom, my boy, too. They say you must let them fix your vittles during the trip. You'll like Mrs.

Crane—she's quite different from old Lije, but she's managed to put up with him for forty years, which is something to the old hardshell's credit, I reckon."

Slade cared for his horse and then repaired to the Cranes' fire near their wagon. Mrs. Crane proved to be ample, motherly and placid. She welcomed Slade with a ready smile.

"My! What a tall boy you are!" she exclaimed. "Sit right down and make yourself at home," she added hospitably. "You've met Lije, I believe. Don't mind him. He thinks the Good Lord put him on earth to tell Him how to run things down here. Personally, I think the Lord is capable of handling things without any advice from Lije."

"Tildy," said the Reverend Crane, with an attempt at severity that didn't impress, "you are blasphemous."

"Oh, I don't know," replied Mrs. Crane. "I'm sure the Lord must have a sense of humor, otherwise He wouldn't have made us as we are. Don't you think so, Mr. Slade?"

"I certainly do," Slade answered. "If He didn't, He could hardly be expected to put up with us."

"See?" said Mrs. Crane, twinkling her eyes at her husband. Old Lije regarded his wife, and for an instant Slade had a glimpse of the very human spirit behind his ascetic mask. And from that moment on, he had no more forebodings in regard to Elijah Crane.

Old Lije said grace in a sonorous voice that Slade felt sure must have reached the heavens at least.

By the time he was on his third cup of coffee, he had become almost amiable.

Settling back after the good meal, Slade rolled a cigarette and stretched out comfortably, his back against a tree. Soon he was surrounded by a group of youngsters asking innumerable questions, which he answered smilingly.

"He's sure got a way with the kids," chuckled Van Worthington. "He's got 'em spellbound."

"Because he has the understanding heart," Mrs. Crane said softly. "The strongest and bravest are always the gentlest."

Little Tom, Van Worthington's son, came forward timidly, holding a small guitar.

"Uncle Walt," he said. "Dad says you can do anything; maybe you can tune this for me? I can play a few chords, but I can't tune it."

Smiling, Slade took the instrument and deftly tuned it. Then he ran his fingers over the strings with crisp power and played several selections for his small audience.

"Gee!" exclaimed little Tom. "You *can* play!"

"Sing us a cowboy song, Uncle Walt," a piping voice cried.

Slade played a soft prelude, then threw back his black head and sang a rollicking old ballad of the range. The children clapped and cheered, and demanded another, and yet another. And as his great golden baritone-bass pealed and thundered through the shadows of evening, a silent ring of the farmers and their wives gathered about him to listen entranced.

"How about a hymn, Brother?" somebody called as he paused. "We ain't had a real singfest since we left Kentucky."

Slade thought a moment, then his voice rolled forth again in the words of a stirring old hymn.

> Onward, Christian soldiers,
> Marching as to war. . . .

Voice after voice took up the refrain, until the mesa quivered with the vibrating melody. And as the magic stilled, Slade's keen ears heard old Elijah Crane mutter to Worthington: "If he could only see the Light, what an evangelist he would make!"

Without looking up, Slade said, "One can be a better evangelist by the example of his own life than by telling others what to do."

Once again, Elijah Crane appeared unable to find words with which to answer.

Slade gave the guitar back to little Tom and the children were hustled off to bed.

"You'll sleep in my wagon, of course," said Worthington.

"Be glad to when the weather is bad," Slade

replied. "But on a fine night like this, I prefer my blanket under the stars."

"Good night, then," said Worthington. "See you in the morning." Slade moved from under the tree and sat down with his back against a rock, from where he had a better view of the sky.

Out of the moonlight she came, to pause before him. Slade remembered that when he saw her that morning it had been with the golden glory of the sunshine behind her. Now it was the soft and silvery beauty of the moon. What a picture she made! Poised like a bird ready to take flight! Instead of the denim shirt and overalls she had affected that morning, she wore a simple dress of some clinging material that set off to advantage the alluring lines of her small figure. The glossy curls of her short dark hair clustered about the perfect oval of her face and enhanced the scarlet witchery of her mouth. Her eyes were great dark pools fringed by thick black lashes under her arched black brows.

"May I sit down?" she asked. "I'd like to talk to you."

"Plenty of room," he replied.

She sat down on the ground in front of him, cupped her chin in one pink palm and regarded him steadfastly for a moment.

"I wonder why I did what you told me to this morning," she said.

"Because I told you to, I suppose," he replied. She thought that over for a moment.

"But why did you tell me to?"

"For your own safety; the last wagon in a train is no place for a lone woman."

She tossed her curly head. "I can take care of myself."

"Perhaps, with civilized people," he conceded. "But not with the kind of characters you could conceivably go up against here."

"I have a rifle in my wagon, and I can shoot," she said pointedly.

"Under certain circumstances it would be best for you to use it on yourself," he told her grimly.

"What do you mean by that?"

"Miss Austin," he said, "we are going into a wild country in which there are wild men, some with more characteristics of beasts than men."

"I have always heard that Western men are chivalrous," she said.

"Are all Kentuckians?" he countered.

"Well, no," she was forced to admit.

"The same obtains here," he said. "Usually a nice woman is perfectly safe here, but not always. And the fact that she is a nice woman sometimes makes her position more dangerous. A nice woman brings a better price as a—slave."

The blue eyes widened. "Do you mean to say that women are sold as slaves?"

"A genteel word for it; it has happened."

"And do you believe this train is in danger?"

"Any train traversing the country ahead of us is in danger, unless proper precautions are taken," he replied. "This is a big train and a strong one and should get through without trouble, but we will take no chances."

"I see," she said slowly. "I am beginning to understand why you made me move ahead this morning; but I don't like being told what to do."

"Most children don't," he answered.

"I'm not a child," she snapped. "I'm almost twenty."

"So young?" he said. "I'd have given you thirty, at least."

She glared at him. Then abruptly a dimple showed at the corner of her red mouth. She stood up lithely.

"I think," she said, "that you are more dangerous than the men you were talking about."

"What do you mean by that?" he demanded.

"Find the answer for yourself," she retorted, and was gone.

FIVE

When Slade awoke at sunrise, the farmers were already astir, for they were early birds in the real sense of the word. By the time he had washed up at the stream and had cared for Shadow, Mrs. Crane was calling him to breakfast.

After the meal, Slade gave some orders to Worthington. "Have the water barrels filled to the brim, and every other utensil that will hold water," he directed.

"Going to hit dry country?" asked the farmer.

"Not particularly," Slade replied. "Van, I have something to tell you. I didn't bother you with it before, for I knew very well that you people were going ahead, regardless. There is a bad bunch operating in this section, their chief objective wagon trains. Two trains have recently been burned, the men killed, the women and children carried off. People think they are renegade Indians, and the devils foster the idea, but they are not. However, they employ some Indian raiding methods, effectively. A fire arrow onto the canvas top of a wagon and you have a blaze in no time, and unless you are prepared to extinguish the fire at once, you are in trouble. Let a few wagons be fired and the women and children panicked and the whole train is thrown into confusion and is easy prey despite a numerical advantage. Understand?"

"Guess I do," replied Worthington. "Okay, we'll be ready for the skunks. I'm not worried, with you handling things."

"Hope your confidence won't be misplaced," Slade said, with a smile.

"It won't," Worthington declared, positively, and went to relay the order to the wagons.

While the train was being made ready, Slade rode to the edge of the mesa and again studied the terrain ahead. He had a fairly good idea as to where the Valley of Lost Stars was located, but in that wild tangle of mountains and deserts and valleys it might take considerable searching to root it out of the maze.

He drew an imaginary line from the jagged mass of the Glass Mountains on the north, to the far-off hazy and many-colored ramparts of the Chisos on the south; and another line southwest, from where he sat his horse, to the Carazone Peaks beyond the horizon. Somewhere in the neighborhood of where the two lines crossed, south of Persimmon Gap and to the west, should be his goal. He glanced back and saw that the farmers were awaiting the word to advance.

Slade altered the disposition of the wagons somewhat before starting the train down the sag. He drew the wains closer together in single-file marching order and directed that they stay that way. The horsemen he told to ride on either side of the trail, as much as a mile distant if possible, and to keep a sharp lookout for anything that appeared suspicious.

"If you sight something, don't go barging into it," he ordered. "You may well find yourselves in a trap. Hightail back to the train with the information. Worthington, keep a watch on them so far as you can and make sure they do as they are told. After we get down the sag, you stay to the rear and scan the back trail frequently. Everything understood? Okay. And remember, in this sort of country a mistake can easily be your last. Get going!"

He reined his horse aside and watched the train roll past, satisfied with its formation. When Mary Austin's wagon reached him, he paced Shadow alongside it.

"Good morning," he said. "Sleep well?"

"Wonderfully," she replied, smiling. "I always do. And you? In Van's wagon, I suppose."

"No," he said. "By that rock where you left me."

Her eyes widened. "But weren't you cold?" she asked. "And—lonesome?"

"I had my blanket," he said. "And if one learns to live with one's self, one is never lonesome. Besides, I had my horse, and the stars, both good company."

"I think I can understand that," she said slowly. "Do you often do it?"

"Quite often, in nice weather," he answered. "Sometimes when the weather isn't nice, through necessity; a cowhand gets used to such things."

"I think," she said slowly, "that you are not a cowhand, although perhaps you have been one, at times."

"What makes you think so?" he asked. She shrugged daintily and veered the leaders a trifle.

"Woman's intuition, perhaps," she replied. "Yes, I think I can understand your content in being alone; I've been alone myself for a while now, and I don't find it so terrible. Perhaps I'll try sleeping under the stars myself. Although," she glanced over her shoulder, "my wagon is warm and cozy."

"Yes?" he said.

"Yes. Why do you laugh?"

"Because," he replied, his eyes dancing, "because I think I've found the answer to my question of last night."

Under his regard, she blushed, and the silken curtain of her lashes swept down. Then they raised and she looked him squarely in the eyes.

"I hope so," she said softly.

Slade laughed again, waved his hand and rode on to the head of the column, where he found Van Worthington awaiting him.

"And now I suppose you want me to drop back to the rear?" the farmer said.

"That's right," Slade told him. "From now on I ride several miles in front of the train. If there's anything off-color in the wind I may be able to spot it."

He was tightening his grip on the split reins and about to give Shadow the word, when old Elijah Crane rode up beside him.

"It is the post of danger, is it not?" he said. "I'll ride with you, if I may."

Slade looked him up and down with his cold eyes, doubtfully.

"It's no chore for anybody not used to the work," he said. "I appreciate your offer, but the chances are I'll do better alone."

"Listen," said Crane, "I was born and brought up in the Kentucky mountains. I know the hills and the woods. I've stalked game plenty. And men, too," he added grimly. "My folks were feudists."

Slade bit back a smile. He wondered how the old fellow reconciled his piety with feuding.

"All right," he said. "We ride together."

All day long they rode side by side, saying little, carefully observing the movements of birds and little animals, probing thickets and ridges with keen eyes, constantly scanning the horizon for signs of smoke.

"Everything looks very peaceful," Crane remarked.

"Yes, too darn peaceful," Slade replied. "I'm always suspicious of the Bend country when it's overly peaceful; we've got to be careful."

"The Lord will care for His own," old Lije observed piously.

"Yes, He will," Slade agreed. "But that doesn't absolve us of the responsibility of looking after ourselves. That's our share of the bargain. We mustn't expect Him to do for us what we are capable of doing for ourselves."

Old Lije rubbed his chin, and remarked, "You are a very bold young man, and talk, I think, a little wildly."

"Heterodoxy has been styled so before," Slade replied.

"Hmmm!" said Crane, who was evidently not uneducated. "Heterodoxy: contrary to or different from some acknowledged standard, as the Bible."

"Or the generally accepted interpretation, *by men,* of the Bible," Slade countered.

Old Lije rubbed his chin again and did not continue the discussion.

Toward evening they came upon a low mesa somewhat similar to the one they had quitted earlier in the day. There was a spring of water, and a wide view to the south and west.

"A good spot for the camp," Slade said. "We'll await the train here."

After the wagons had been properly arranged, this time in a circle, Slade walked to the edge of the mesa, and leaning against a shoulder-high boulder, gazed at that marvel of loveliness, a sunset over the Big Bend.

He heard her approach, although her small feet, encased in beaded moccasins, made hardly any sound on the ground.

"Hello?" he said, without looking around. "A

wonderful sunset tonight, and a fine place from which to view it."

"Have you got eyes in the back of your head?" she demanded as she paused beside him.

"I can't see back there, but I don't think so," he replied. Turning, he reached down, encircled her slender waist with his hands and hoisted her to the flat top of the boulder.

"Good gracious!" she exclaimed. "No wonder that poor horse didn't have a chance when you took hold of him."

"You're hardly as heavy as the horse," he said, smiling up at her.

"I should hope not," she replied. "I'm not too small, though."

"I guess you'll get by," he said.

For some time they were silent, absorbing the tremendous prospect spread before their eyes.

"It is a wild and terrible land, but it uplifts one like the surge and thunder of a storm," she said at length. "I always thought the Kentucky mountains grand and rugged, but they are nothing compared to these. It will be wonderful to live with them."

"A poet's dream of beauty frozen into stone," he said.

The girl gazed down at him, wonderingly. What *could* he be, anyhow! Imagine a cowhand saying a thing like that!

Her eyes grew wistful. He was one with this

wild land. One with its rugged grandeur, its great distances, its sweeping plains and its soaring mountains. Free, untamed! One with the lonely heights. She sighed.

The sun set in splendor behind the crags of the Del Nortes. The sky flamed scarlet and gold, softened to rose, faded to steely gray. The shadows gathered. And in the west a great star glowed and trembled.

"Help me down," she said. "I promised the Cranes to have supper with them tonight; we mustn't keep them waiting."

He reached up and lifted her gently from the boulder. For a moment he held her close. Their lips met, clung. She giggled as he dropped her lightly to her feet.

"I fear the Reverend wouldn't approve," she said. "Yes, and I also fear you *have* found the answer to your question. Oh, well! 'Dead yesterday and unborn tomorrow!' 'Gather ye rosebuds while ye may!' "

They walked back to the wagon, very slowly.

At the Crane fire they enjoyed an excellent and very pleasant repast. Under the influence of Leela's gay company, old Lije became almost human and Slade wondered if under certain circumstances he might not lose some of his righteousness.

He walked with Leela to her wagon, where they paused.

"I suppose you plan to sleep beside that big rock where we watched the sunset?" she said.

"Yes," he replied.

She was silent for a moment, then, "The stars *are* beautiful tonight."

"Very beautiful," he agreed, smiling down at her.

She returned his kiss, warmly; but she did not say good night.

SIX

The next day, when Slade paused at Leela's wagon, Mrs. Crane, who mothered everybody she thought needed mothering, was there.

"She's a gem," the old lady told the Ranger. "Look! her wagon's already all straightened up, her bed made. You wouldn't think it had been slept in. My, honey," she added to Leela, "what a pretty color you have this morning; your cheeks are like roses!"

Slade smiled at Leela and went to consult with Van Worthington.

Again Elijah Crane rode with Slade, well in advance of the wagons. The Ranger was even more alert than the day before, for now they were getting into the grim fastnesses of the Big Bend. On their right were the Del Norte mountains, and farther south the beginning of the Santiago chain, a part of the broken backbone of the Rockies, with Yellow House Peak and the twin black peaks of Dove Mountain on their left and some miles farther south.

"We're heading for Persimmon Gap, a pass in the Santiago Range," Slade told his companion. "Through the gap runs the Comanche Trail, blazed by raiding Indians from the South Plains on their way to Mexico. Farther to the south on our left are the Sierra Del Caballo Muerto, locally called by its English translation, the Dead Horse Mountains. In that range are the real badlands of the Big Bend, where water is almost unobtainable except in natural rock depressions which catch rain water."

"A mighty bad country," remarked Crane.

"Yes, it is," Slade agreed. "But beyond the Gap we turn more to the west. Down there the trail forks. The west fork is not much more than a snake track and easily missed. And that track should lead to the vicinity of the Valley of Lost Stars, which I think I can locate without too much difficulty. By the route we're following, we'll hit the Comanche before so very long, some miles south of Marathon, the railroad town."

Rugged and still more rugged grew the terrain over which they passed, with gulleys and ridges, draws and wide hollows. In many places the chaparral was a thorny tangle. In others there was nothing but naked rock, scarred and rent and fissured. They were passing through the Marathon Basin, one of the oldest sedimentary formations on the North American Continent. And as is the way with age, it was vastly "wrinkled" and puckered.

Slade and Crane had paused for a moment to breathe their horses behind a litter of boulders near a thicket. Suddenly Crane uttered a sharp exclamation. Slade had already seen it and was gazing intently into the northwest.

Shimmering darkly in the sun, a slender column of smoke had soared up from the crest of a hill which they had passed half an hour or so before. It broke from its base, floated away into the blue of the sky. A rolling puff soared upward, was followed by a second streamer, then a series of puffs.

"What is it?" asked Crane.

"Smoke signals—Indian talk, or supposed to be," Slade replied, his eyes still fixed on the distant puffs and streamers. "They use a sort of telegraph code; the streaks correspond to dashes, the puffs to dots. Yes, it's supposed to be Indian smoke talk; but I am familiar enough with the smoke talk to know that what that fellow is sending up is nothing but gibberish. But," he added thoughtfully, "it may mean something to some others of the bunch down this way."

"Do you think they're talking about us?" asked Crane.

"That's what I'd like to know for sure," Slade replied grimly. "I've a very strong notion they are. Rather, that somebody is sending a signal to somebody else that we are here. I'm afraid we're in for trouble. Quite likely they spotted us crossing one of the ridges. That hill was too far from the trail to do any shooting from it, and the ground between it and the trail was open, you'll recall. So they're sending a signal to somebody else who may be within shooting distance somewhere around; that's what I'm afraid of."

"What shall we do?" asked Crane.

"Nothing," Slade answered. "It's up to them to make the play. We'll wait, that's all we can do right now. We can't risk hightailing back to the train; they may be between it and us, and we're very likely outnumbered.

"I wish those darn brush-covered ridges down there weren't so close. I think we'd better hole up the horses in that thicket over to the left. These rocks will give us some protection, but they don't hide the horses."

They forced the horses into the dense growth, then returned to their post of observation behind the rocks, for the thicket was on slightly lower ground and did not afford a good view of the surrounding terrain.

"There in the brush they could surround us without us being aware of it until too late," Slade explained.

The smoke signals had ceased; the sky shone stainless blue. Nowhere could they see signs of movement; the minutes dragged past.

Slade kept watching the brush-covered ridges, especially one almost directly in front of them and too close for comfort. He wished he could get a glimpse down the far side of the sag, and had about made up his mind to a quick dash across the open, when Crane arose from his crouch to ease his cramped limbs.

"Look out!" the Ranger roared, hurling himself against his companion.

From the ridge crest wisped smoke. The clang of a rifle rang loud in the silence. Elijah Crane threw up his hands, reeled and flopped to the ground behind a boulder.

Slade threw his Winchester forward, snapped a shot at the smoke puff and hurled himself down. The growth topping the ridge was violently agitated. A dark figure plunged over the lip, rolled down the slope a little way and was still.

"Got one of the hellions!" Slade exulted. "Wonder if they did for poor Crane."

A moment later, however, he was reassured on that point. Behind him, old Lije was grunting and sputtering. Slade did not dare take his eyes off the ridge.

"Just burned my head with a slug, thanks to you," Crane replied to the anxious whisper he breathed over his shoulder. "How'd you spot him?"

"Saw the sun glint on his rifle barrel when he shifted it to line sights," Slade whispered answer. "Keep down and keep quiet, and don't do any shooting. Let them think they got one of us; it may help. We are in a tough spot."

Rifles were cracking back of the ridge. Bullets chipped fragments from the boulders, ricocheted and whined off into space. Slade cast an anxious glance to right and left. If the devils managed to surround them, they were done. However, the ridge extended for a long distance in either direction, with open ground before it.

But if they were held in their precarious position until dark there was a good chance they'd be surrounded and finished off. The train, Slade felt sure, would make camp before continuing this far. He had cautioned Worthington to do so well before dark at any desirable spot.

He began counting the shots that were fired almost in volleys. "I don't think there are more than four of them over there," he told Crane. "I've a notion we can outfox them. Chances are they feel sure they got one of us. I'll make a quick dash for the thicket and the horses. Very likely they'll try to rush me. Then you can down them when they break cover."

"No," countered Crane. "I'll make the dash. I got long legs and I'm a mighty fast runner, while you're the faster and better shot."

Before Slade could object, he was on his feet and scudding across the open space, ducking and dodging.

From the ridge came a chorus of yells and a banging of rifles. Bullets whipped about Crane, whirled his hat from his head, ripped the sleeve of his coat; but he ran on. Had the dry-gulchers taken careful aim they could hardly have missed him; but they fired wildly in their excitement. Crane was halfway to the thicket when there was a crashing in the brush and four yelling figures leaped into view and raced down the slope.

Slade dropped his Winchester, whipped his sixes from their holsters and leaped to his feet; the big Colts let go with a rattling crash.

Two of the attackers went down, to lie like bundles of old clothes. A third reeled, stumbled, and fell; then the hammers of Slade's guns clicked on empty shells.

Elijah Crane whirled around as Slade dived for his Winchester. The charging dry-gulcher gave a yell and fired his rifle; but Crane stood rock still and took careful aim, Kentucky-style. The long gun boomed and the dry-gulcher went heels over head like a plugged rabbit. Old Lije let out an exultant whoop and ran to rejoin Slade, who was scanning the silent ridge crest.

"I think that's all of them," he told Crane as the latter came panting up to the rocks. "We'll have a look at the bodies; but wait a minute."

He stood gazing at the motionless forms, rifle ready.

"They're dead, all right," he said at length.

"How do you know for sure?" Crane asked.

"Sun's shining on their faces, and it's still hot, and they're not sweating," Slade explained. "A dead man does not sweat. Just the same, don't take any chances with them. That sort, only wounded and playing possum for an opportunity to take one of us with him when he takes the Big Jump, is dangerous as a broken-back rattler."

For another moment he studied the ridge crest. Finally, satisfied that no danger lay there, he said, "Let's go."

"Indians, ain't they?" Crane asked as they paused beside the motionless forms. "Faces almost black, and their clothes sure look like Indian clothes, don't they?"

Slade shook his head. "No, they are not Indians," he said. "They did a pretty good job of dyeing their faces to resemble the red-black of the Apache, but they slipped a mite on costume. If they were Apaches as they pretend to be, they would be wearing loincloths, high boot-moccasins, a necklace of bear claws, a dirty white turban, and a single eagle feather on their heads. These beaded moccasins, hide britches and fringed shirt are the get-up of a Tonkawa young warrior. And there never was a Tonkawa Indian this far west. Watch, now."

He reached down, ripped the fringed shirt open. White skin showed through the tear.

"See?" Slade remarked sententiously. "I wish they were Indians, instead of what they are. Indians, contrary to popular belief, are not noted for smartness. Their methods are direct and not hard to anticipate. These are white men of better than average intelligence, and the sidewinder who heads the outfit is smart as a treeful of owls, also giving owls credit for brains they don't really possess."

Old Lije clucked in his throat and shook his head. "They would have sure fooled me," he admitted.

"Just as they have been fooling a lot of other people," Slade observed.

Crane shook his head again. "I've a plumb notion it is *you* who's smart as the treeful of owls you spoke of," he said.

"It's just that I've had some experience with this sort of thing," Slade deprecated. "You'll note, too, that there are pockets in the britches," he pointed out. "That's not the Indian way of packing things."

Swiftly and deftly, he searched the dead men, discovering nothing of significance save a surprisingly large amount of money.

"Hellions have been doing very well by themselves," he commented. "Take this dinero and put it in your common treasury, if you have one, or do whatever you like with it. No, I don't want any, and I've a notion you folks can use it."

"We can," admitted Crane, pocketing the bills and coin. "Now what?"

"Now we're hightailing back to the train," Slade decided. "Wait, though; there must be horses somewhere close. We'll get the rigs off them so they can fend for themselves. The rest of this paraphernalia, including the guns, we'll leave. If they're still here when the train comes along, the boys can pick them up if they wish to."

They located the four horses, tethered in the brush, and turned them loose. Slade studied the brands a moment.

"Interesting," he commented. "A Circle W; that's a Panhandle brand. Critters are a long ways from home; stolen, very likely."

It *was* interesting, he thought. His feud with Veck Sosna had started in the Panhandle. Just another corroboration of his belief that Sosna was the head of the raiders.

"Now let's get out of here," he told his companion. "Before some more of the devils come snooping around. Next time the odds might be a mite lopsided."

"Maybe they will have learned a lesson from what happened today and leave us alone hereafter," observed Crane.

"Not a chance," Slade replied. "We've thrown down the gauntlet and the hellion who heads the bunch will never cease trying to even the score so long as he has a follower left. Well, we'll see. We know what to expect now and will be prepared against it. Very likely the next try will be for the train; we've got to watch our step."

Backtracking swiftly, after a while they came on the train, which had already made camp at a favorable spot. As Slade had directed, the wagons had been arranged in a circle, which would make them easier to defend were they attacked.

Great was the excitement of the farmers when regaled with an account of the day's happenings. Old Lije was loud in his praise of Slade.

"Never saw such shooting," he declared. "Didn't seem to take aim at all; just pulled his guns quicker'n a flash and cut loose. And down the skunks went.

"But I got one," he declared proudly. "He sure went conflutin'; end over end. No, Tildy, I ain't hurt, thanks to Slade; just a scratch. But if he hadn't taken time to shove me aside before looking after himself, I reckon it would be a different story."

"I shouldn't let you out of my sight," Leela told the Ranger, severely. "You're not to be trusted by yourself; I think you go looking for trouble."

"How about yourself?" he asked smilingly.

"Oh, I guess I did, too," she admitted. "Rather nice trouble, though."

"I'm glad you think so," he said.

"I wouldn't think I'd need to tell you—again," she retorted, the dimple showing.

"Again, and yet again, please!"

Leela giggled, and changed the subject.

SEVEN

The following morning they struck the Comanche Trail and the going was much better; but it was a slow drag up the long and twisting slope to Persimmon Gap and they made camp in the south mouth of the Pass, from whence they had a good view of the distant Chisos Mountains. Blue, red, purple, and yellow, they bulked in a serrated mass on the horizon to the southwest, rugged, aloof, a cluster of major and minor peaks dominating the tip of the Big Bend.

"Their misty appearance is due to an atmospheric haze," Slade explained to Worthington, who gazed in awe at their sky-piercing beauty. "Which is given as one interpretation of their name—that is derived from an Apache word meaning ghostly. In long-past geologic ages they were thrust up through sedimentary limestone beds. Erosion from the uplift has covered the adjacent desert with rubble which makes for hard going. The limestone is not again exposed until it outcrops in the walls of three great canyons which the Rio Grande has carved for itself through intervening rock ranges. A most interesting formation."

"Sounds that way, as much as I can understand what you're saying," replied Worthington. "Anyhow, they're sure worth coming clean across Texas to see. What are those mountains down there to the south and a lot nearer?"

"Those are the Rosillos. Those much farther on are the Christmas Mountains and the Corazones Peaks—the Heart Mountains. After we cross Dog Creek and Santiago Creek and pass the Rosillos, we turn more to the west on the old track I told you about. Then, not so very far off, is the mouth of the Valley of Lost Stars. I'm pretty sure I can locate it. At Boraches Spring, about eight miles from the foot of the sag ahead, is a ranch, or used to be, in a grass-grown valley. I've a notion we may be able to obtain some information there."

"Guess we can, if you say so," said Worthington. "You seem to know everything."

"I've been down through this section a few times," Slade explained.

Around noon the following day, Slade called a halt. "Take it easy and have something to eat," he told the farmers. "I'm going to ride over to that ranchhouse—just about three miles to the southwest—and see if I can learn something. Van, you're the head of this shebang, so you come along with me."

Riding in the shadow of the Rosillos, they had

no difficulty locating the ranchhouse, which sat in the mouth of the valley. As they approached, they saw an old Mexican standing on the veranda and when they pulled up beside the porch, he started, removed his sombrero and bowed low to Slade.

"*Capitán!*" he exclaimed. "Praise be to *Dios!* This is indeed a welcome sight to my old eyes!"

Slade smiled, and replied to the greeting in Spanish. As he was speaking, an elderly, pleasant-faced man stepped from the open door.

"Howdy?" he said. "Anything I can do for you fellers?"

Slade explained their mission. The rancher whistled.

"Valley of Lost Stars," he repeated. "Espantosa Valley we call it hereabouts. Ain't you scared of the ghosts? Felipe here and all the other Mexicans swear that hole is haunted."

Slade smilingly shook his head.

"El Halcón fears not ghosts, or evil spirits, or *El Diablo* himself," Felipe put in. "Why? Because his heart is clean."

"Thank you, Felipe," Slade said, his cold eyes abruptly very kind.

"If Felipe stands up for you, you must be all right," chuckled the rancher. "Never knew him to be wrong. Light off for coffee and a snack. My name's Butterick, Sam Butterick. I don't think I caught your handles."

Slade supplied them and they shook hands.

"Felipe, take the cayuses to the barn and give them a helpin' of oats," directed the hospitable Butterick. "Then hustle back and throw a surroundin' together."

"I'll go along and help," volunteered Worthington, who knew that Shadow would allow no stranger to put a hand on him unless properly introduced by his master. As he and Felipe headed for the barn, he remarked,

"You seem to know my friend."

"Senõr," said the old Mexican, "he is El Halcón, the friend of the lowly, the champion of all who are wronged, mistreated, sorrowful. Evil flees before him. You are fortunate to have such a man for an *amigo*, one whom the hand of *El Dios* has touched."

"I believe every word you say," declared Worthington. "I've got good reason to."

Meanwhile, Slade and Butterick had entered the living room of the ranchhouse. The rancher waved him to a chair.

"Take a load off your feet while I put the coffee on to heat," he said. "Felipe will take over when he gets back from the barn; he's my cook, and I swear by him."

"Espantosa Valley, eh?" he remarked when he returned. "Keep following that track, which starts a few miles farther down the Comanche, and you can't miss it, once you know what to look for. Otherwise you'd very likely pass it by. The track runs right past a couple of big tall hills on the south. There's a narrow pass between them and it looks like it runs on into the hills, but it don't. A mile farther on and the pass opens out into the valley. It's a hidden valley, all right, like lots of 'em in the Bend. It's brush-grown but I've a notion it would grow good crops if it's cleared. Yep, they should make out okay. It's not good range so they won't be having trouble with the cowmen of the section. State land, of course, and I figure they can get title for almost nothing. Not overly far to Marathon and the railroad, as you know. Yep, it should be okay for them. About twenty miles of going from where you camped. How you been making out so far?"

The rancher's face darkened as Slade recounted their misadventure with the psuedo-Indians.

"That bunch has been raising the devil all through the Bend," he declared. "We've all been losing cows and figure they're to blame. White men, you say? We all figured it was a bunch of wild Indians from Mexico. No wonder we haven't been able to run the hellions down; we've been looking for Indians all the time."

"The same applies to folks over around Morton," Slade said. "Yes, it's a bad bunch, and there won't be any peace until they are cleaned out."

Worthington entered and soon afterward Felipe

74

called them to the snack he had prepared, which proved to be really an excellent meal.

"He can do more with nothing in the shortest time of any hellion I ever knew," Butterick declared proudly.

"We got a lucky break," Slade remarked after they said good-by to their host and headed back to the wagons. "Otherwise we might have wasted a lot of time hunting for the place. When a valley is hidden in the Big Bend it's really hidden. As it is, we should have no trouble locating it. We'll roll as soon as we reach the camp—quite a few hours of daylight left—and even with the going rough, we should reach the valley some time tomorrow."

"Smart of you to think of paying that feller a visit," said Worthington. "He's okay, and that old cook of his is fine. Sorry we didn't get to meet his hands, but he said they were all out on the range. Looks like, after folks at Morton and him, that cattle fellers ain't always so bad, after all."

"You'll find most of them pretty decent folks," Slade replied. "That goes for people most everywhere, a lot more good than bad."

"Guess that's right," conceded Worthington. "Anyhow, I'm getting to believe it is."

When they arrived at the camp, they found the wagons ready to roll. Slade rode directly in front of the train, now, constantly scanning the ground to the west. It was nearly sunset when he announced, "Here it is. Not much of a trail, but I think the wagons can take it. Best as I recall, it's most level ground from here on and the going shouldn't be too bad. And right here is a pretty good spot to camp."

The night passed without incident and at daybreak the train entered the almost unnoticeable side track and continued on its way. Again Slade and old Lije rode well in advance of the train, to look over conditions and search out a suitable spot for the night encampment.

The contours of the land had changed somewhat. Although the going was rather rough, there were frequent open and level spaces sparsely brush-grown and with considerable grass.

"Not particularly good range, but cattle could subsist on it," Slade commented. "Sooner or later it will all be taken up and put to use. So far, however, there's plenty of good grazing land available. You're lucky in getting in on the ground floor in your valley, as it were, for as Butterick said, with the brush cleared away it will grow grass. Only a matter of time until somebody in search of land would figure that out and take over, once the good pasture is filled."

Hour after hour they rode steadily and the afternoon was waning when they reached a spot Slade decided would make a good camping site.

"We might as well wait here and take it easy

for a spell," he told his companion. "Give the horses a chance to fill up and drink at the creek. No, don't take the rig off yet—just loosen the cinches and flip out the bit. Always have your cayuse handy in case you might want to use him. We'll unsaddle after the train shows."

Making themselves comfortable, they enjoyed a leisurely smoke. Slade kept glancing at the sun. After his second cigarette he stood up and gazed along the back track, which ran straight for more than a mile and was clearly visible. He rolled another cigarette, smoked it halfway down. Then abruptly he pinched it out and cast it aside.

"Seems to me the train should have showed by now," he remarked. "Tighten your cinches and let's ride to meet it."

He did not say more, being reluctant to alarm his companion needlessly, but he was getting a mite bothered about the wagons. Looked like some accident might have held them up.

And as they topped ridge after ridge, with no sign of the big wains, he became acutely nervous.

"What's that?" Crane suddenly exclaimed. From somewhere ahead came a faint crackling, like thorns burning briskly under a pot.

"Outsmarted, that's what!" Slade exclaimed bitterly. "I should have stayed with the train, and maybe I could have prevented it. They kept tabs on us, allowed us to get far ahead and then tackled the train at some favorable spot. That's rifle fire you hear. Come on! I only hope we're not too late."

He sent Shadow charging forward. Crane's big roan labored valiantly to catch up, but Slade had to curb his mount a little to keep from leaving the farmer behind.

"Yes, plain outsmarted," Slade repeated. "And I should have known better, knowing the man I'm dealing with as I do."

"Don't over blame yourself, son," old Lije consoled. "Anyhow, I think you got us started back in time to lend a hand that may turn the tide. The boys are fighters and will put up a tough battle. I'm sure we'll be in time."

"I hope so," Slade said. "Trail, Shadow!"

The sound of rifle fire grew louder. As they toiled up a long slope, faint whoops and screeches reached their ears.

"Still keeping up the deception," Slade muttered. "A pretty good imitation of Apache battle cries. Ease up a bit; guns are sounding mighty loud. I've a notion they're just the other side of the sag."

The crest of the slope was crowned by tall brush. They topped the rise, eased their horses to a swift walk, slowed them still more as they reached the final fringe of growth. Cautiously they peered forth, the din of rifle fire and the fiendish yelling loud in their ears.

At the foot of the low rise and less than three

hundred yards distant, the wagons were drawn together in a rough circle in an open space dotted with clumps of thicket. And racing and swooping around the train, riding their horses Apache-style, were fully a score of "Indians." Leaning low in their saddles, shielded by the necks of their horses, they fired their rifles and uttered bloodcurdling yells. Answering shots smoked and flamed between the spokes of the wagon wheels. A couple of sprawled forms on the grass attested to the accuracy of the defenders' fire.

From the circling ranks whizzed a flaming arrow. Another and another. One quivered in the canvas top of a wagon. A flicker almost instantly became a spreading flame. Then water dashed upward inside the wagon. The fire hissed out in a whortle of smoke. But now another wagon was blazing. Slade could hear the screams of terrified women and children. And the fire arrows were whining in a shower.

"Next will be panic, and utter confusion!" Slade exclaimed. "Come on, Crane, we've got to stop it." He and the farmer flung themselves from their saddles, sliding their rifles free. Side by side they stood, legs apart, feet firmly planted. Smoke spurted from the rock-steady muzzles.

Slade shot in true Texas style, the lever of his Winchester a flickering blur as it ejected the spent shells. Elijah Crane was the Kentucky mountaineer. He took steady aim, fired slowly, but with methodical sureness.

Two "Indians" whirled from their saddles. Another, and another. Still another howled with pain and clutched at his blood-spouting shoulder. The rifles roared and two more went down.

That was enough, and too much, for the raiders. Thrown into confusion by the unexpectedness of the attack and the appalling accuracy of the two rifles, they howled curses in good English, whirled their horses and raced away from the train, dodging in and out between the thickets and stands of brush. The defenders of the wagons raised a roar of triumph and fired the faster. Slade and Crane sent final shots after the fleeing dry-gulchers, with the result that one more dropped from his saddle before they were shielded by the growth and out of range.

Slade and Crane remounted and rode down the slope. The farmers were streaming from shelter, shouting greetings, Van Worthington in the lead. The fired canvas had been drenched to a steaming smolder.

"But if you fellers hadn't showed up when you did and took 'em in the rear, we'd have been goners," Worthington declared. "Another minute and the wagons would have been burning in every direction. Already the womenfolks and the kids were getting out of control, to say nothing of the horses wanting to run and get away from the fire. Four or five of them were killed. Lucky we got some spares."

"Anybody hurt?" Slade asked.

"Curt Blaine has a busted shoulder, and Jasper Mason's got a hole in his leg," Worthington replied. "Mrs. Crane is looking after them. Two or three more got skinned up a little, nothing to worry about.

"But they killed two of the outriders," he added sadly. "Shot 'em when they swooped out of the brush over to the north. We heard the shooting and I remembered what you told me to do and got the wagons into a circle before they were too close. But things were looking bad when you fellers got here. We ain't used to moving targets, and the fire arrows had us bad scared."

"Two killed, you say?" Slade questioned.

"That's right," Worthington replied. "Two of the young fellers. Bad, but it could have been worse. They were unattached. At least they didn't leave widows and fatherless kids."

"May the Lord receive the souls of His servants," prayed Elijah Crane.

"Some of the boys have gone to bring in the bodies," Worthington said. "Now what?"

"First I'll lend Mrs. Crane a hand," Slade said. "While I'm at it, you might collect the carcasses of those hellions we downed; I'll want to look them over. Might as well make camp here, too; not a bad place."

"You don't figure the rest of the skunks will come back?" Worthington asked anxiously.

"Not them," Slade replied. "I figure they got a bellyful that will hold them for a while. We can expect more trouble from them when they get reorganized, but not for a while. They lost seven of their number, and that's enough to give even a big outfit pause."

Worthington began counting on his fingers. "The way I figure it, including those in Morton and the four you and Crane downed the other day, they've lost fourteen altogether. Wonder how many they have left?"

"Perhaps a dozen, I'd guess," Slade replied. "Could be one or two more, including the head of the outfit whom I haven't spotted so far, although he might have been with the bunch today; I wasn't close enough to see who looked like the leader. Now I'll go have a look at the wounded."

A quick examination assured him that the injuries were not serious for such hardy individuals. He smeared the wounds with antiseptic ointment, padded and bandaged them, and left the patients to Mrs. Crane's ministrations. After which he returned to where the bodies of the slain raiders were laid out for his inspection.

All had faces and hands smeared with the dark dye, but opened shirts revealed white skin underneath; although several, Slade felt sure, had some Indian blood and were typical of the

Comancheros of the north Panhandle country. Which gave the Ranger cause for thought.

At his direction, the pockets of the dead men were emptied. Slade gave the heap a close once-over, discovering a number of trinkets such as cowhands carry, but Indians never. Also there were sacks of tobacco and books of papers, which also were not common to the Red men. There was quite a sum of money which he handed over to Worthington.

"I've a notion they'll give up the pretense from now on," was his conclusion. "They'll know very well that we must have uncovered the masquerade and will bother with it no longer. But don't think they'll give up because of this setback; they'll be out to even the score and we've got to keep our eyes open. Tomorrow, with no bad luck, we should reach the valley. There we'll decide on what precautions should be taken against another raid."

The following morning the two slain outriders were buried. Elijah Crane read the service, his sonorous voice intoning the immortal words: "I am the Resurrection and the Light. . . ."

When he had finished and closed his book, he turned to Slade.

"And, brother, if you would lead us in a hymn," he suggested.

Slade nodded. His golden voice rang out in the words of a comforting old hymn he had sung at several such lonely prairie buryings: "Home again from a distant shore. . . ."

After that the wrapped bodies were lowered and the earth shoveled over them and raised to two more of the wasteland's lonely mounds that would stand bare and brown until the new grass was grown to cover them gently with its green loveliness and its proof of life unending after the last long sleep.

EIGHT

The train rolled on. For a while the farmers were somber; but these dwellers from the stern hills were accustomed to death sharp and swift and soon were their repressed but cheerful selves once more.

Slade did not ride ahead of the train, feeling it better that he accompany it, confident that he would not be lured into any such trap as was sprung the day before. Constantly he examined the terrain, alert for anything out of the ordinary, although he hardly expected the dry-gulchers to make another try so soon. More likely they were still licking their wounds, figuratively speaking.

The day wore on, with the train making good progress. It still lacked two hours to sunset when Slade spotted the twin hills of which Sam Butterick, the ranch owner, had spoken. High into the blue of the sky they towered, heavily grown with chaparral and larger trees, and between them was an opening of only a few hundred yards in width that looked to be but a ravine boring into the uplift. But after a mile or so of going, the hills fell back and before them lay the Promised Land!

Turquoise and amethyst, the mountains rose, their cliffs banded with scarlet, russet and marbled white. The gray of the sage and mesquite on the lower slopes was splashed with emerald and jade. White yuccas swayed in the wind like swung censers. Green and yellow mescal plants soared thirty feet into the air to explode in starry white blooms. The graceful wands of octillos rose like the jets of fairy fountains.

A wide valley, walled by mountains that to the south were misty with distance, its floor was grown with low brush, though the hills that swelled upward to the rocky ramparts of the mountains boasted a plenitude of tall trees. Several little streams edged with silver the valley's garment of green. Far to the southwest, one soaring tower-like peak was a column of pulsing rose, its mighty shoulders swathed in royal purple. Overhead the sky was stainless blue, filled with the red-gold light of the westering sun.

Truly it was a Garden of the Lord, awaiting only man to make it perfect.

Man—and a woman—Walt Slade, who had paused beside Leela Austin's wagon, thought.

He wondered did Eve look more fair to Adam than this girl of the hills who, with eyes aglow and parted lips, gazed at the beauty spread before her as if it were the altar-cloth of God's own cathedral.

Well, if so, when he departed from the Garden, Adam most assuredly had taken paradise with him!

Van Worthington's eyes kindled as they roved over the valley. "It's a beauty," he said to Slade. "Worth coming a long way for, worth fighting for, worth suffering for. And we owe it all to you!"

The wagons rolled down the slope to the valley floor, to make camp on the banks of a stream a mile or so distant. When they halted, Elijah Crane dug deep into the turf with his clasp knife. He ran the crumbly earth through his gnarled fingers.

"Rich!" he said. "Mighty rich!" He raised his eyes to the hill slopes. "And plenty of good timber up there for building. Will take work to clear it, but how shall a man profit but by the labor of his hands! 'Thou preparest a table before me.' Blessed be the Lord, the Merciful, the Compassionate, the Just!"

And that, thought Walt Slade, is true piety.

Old Lije noticed the tall Ranger's eyes upon him and rose to his feet.

"Yes, brother, you were right," he said. "The Good Lord will take care of His end of the chore if we'll just take care of ours. Looks like there are times when an old man can learn from a young one, if he'll just listen, and—think."

Slade and Leela ate the evening meal with the Cranes. Afterwards they walked together on the banks of the little stream. She was silent for quite a while, then, "You'll be leaving now?"

"No, not yet," he replied. "I'll stick around for a while; I still have a chore to do in this section."

"You mean those awful men who attacked the wagons?"

"Yes. There will be other wagons coming; the road must be made safe for them."

She shuddered. "You'll be in constant danger."

"Aren't we all, all the time?" he countered lightly. "Eventually the clock strikes for all of us."

"Yes, but is it necessary to shove the hands?"

"Nobody can, any more than one can retard them," he replied. " 'The Moving Finger writes; and having writ moves on.' "

They walked on, again in silence for a while. Overhead the stars bloomed like silver roses in the sky, to look down as in the long ago they had looked down upon the Masterpiece of the new Creation—a man, a maid, and a Garden!

· · ·

The following morning the wagons rolled farther down the valley to a suitable spot for a permanent camp, and the farmers at once got busy. Brush was cleared away, trees were felled. It would not take these hardy pioneers long to make themselves comfortable.

"We'll build Leela a house and clear her land," Worthington told Slade. "You see, one of the first things we'll build as soon as we get sorta settled is a schoolhouse, and Leela will be the teacher. She's got plenty of learning, as no doubt you've found out. We don't want the kids to grow up ignorant.

"That is," he added with a chuckle, "if you don't decide to stay with us, as we sure wish you would. Then I reckon we'd have to look around for another teacher."

Slade smiled and did not comment. He was studying the valley. A moment later he said, "Van, there is one thing you must do, and at once. Post a guard in the mouth of the pass, day and night. It's narrow and two men with rifles can hold it until the rest of you get organized. So long as those devils who raided the train are on the loose you can't afford to relax your vigilance for a moment. They'll try again if they think they have a chance of winning. I think the pass is all you have to fear, but I'm going to make sure; I'm riding the valley to the far end to give it a careful once-over."

"I'll do it," Worthington acceded. "I'll post two of our best shots behind those rocks, and keep 'em there all the time."

"That's right," Slade said. "Horses coming through the pass can be heard quite a ways off. But warn them to be on the lookout for a sneak attack on foot."

Getting the rig on Shadow, he rode south, keeping close to the east wall. Before long he was convinced that the valley was impervious to attack, from that direction at least. The lower slopes were extremely steep and above them were beetling cliffs. From where he rode, it looked like the western slopes and mountains were of a similar formation; but of that he would make sure later.

It took him two hours to reach the far end of the valley. There he turned west, threading his way between the stands of low brush. The south wall also appeared impregnable.

Before he had covered a mile, he came to a great hollow scored deep in the earth. He pulled up on its lip and regarded it curiously. After a bit he chuckled.

"Shadow," he told the big black, "I guess this crack in the hills deserves its name. Not much doubt but that quite a while back, perhaps a hundred years, a mighty big meteor fell here. Yes, a big one, big enough and weighty enough to drive far into the ground, making this hollow while doing so. Go down in there and dig deep enough and you'd find it. Guess this is something they should know over at the University; scientists might find it interesting. Valley of the Lost Stars! Yes, it's rightly named. No wonder the Indians and the Mexican *peones* think the place is haunted. Must have been pretty lively here when that thing struck, and anybody seeing it would think a star really fell. And the story grew in the course of the years. June along, horse, and let's see what else we can learn."

What he did learn, to his satisfaction, was that the valley was really impregnable to attack except by way of the north pass. It was nearly dark when he reached the camp. He felt that the day had been well spent. Tomorrow was another day, and he already had an expedition planned for tomorrow.

In pursuance with the plan, daybreak found him riding through the still gloomy pass. When he reached the open ground beyond, he reined in, rolled a cigarette and smoked leisurely, studying the terrain ahead the while.

"Shadow," he said as he pinched out the butt, "those gents who tackled the wagon train hightailed away from there mighty fast, and I've a notion they left a pretty plain trail. I also have a notion that somewhere between here and Marathon they have a hangout where they get together to plan their deviltry; it's logical that they would have, so we'll just go and see. First stop, where the fight took place."

What had taken the slow-moving wagon train almost a day to cover sped past under Shadow's hoofs in a very short time. It still lacked an hour and more to noon when Slade reined him in on the crest of the low ridge beneath which the battle with the raiders had taken place. He dismounted to stretch his legs, slipped out the bit and loosened the cinches so that Shadow could partake of a surroundin' of grass in comfort. He knew that a little farther on was water, so the big black would not lack for anything. From his saddle pouches he took a couple of sandwiches Leela had prepared for him, and he enjoyed a snack while Shadow filled up on grass and curly mesquite pods. Then he mounted again and rode slowly across the spot where the wagons had met the raiders' fire.

As he expected, the trail they left when they took a hurried departure was plain and continued that way for several miles. Then the dry-gulchers had apparently gotten over their panic and proceeded in a more circumspect manner. However, there were plenty of indications of their passing, which the keen eyes of El Halcón were able to search out.

"Yep, just as I expected," he remarked. "They headed east by north. Bet you they have a hole-up somewhere not far to the north of Persimmon Gap."

After a while the course the fleeing outlaws had taken led to an old and faint trail, grown with scanty patches of grass and low bush. This track continued in a northeasterly direction, but never joined with the Comanche Trail.

"The Comanche is traveled quite a bit and very likely they don't care to be spotted by somebody," Slade explained to Shadow. "They'll have to use the Comanche to get through the Gap, but then they can turn away from it again. Plenty of tracks in this section, for those who know them. The Indians crisscrossed this region in the old days. I think, though, that we'll make camp this side of the pass, at the first good spot we find. Soon be getting dusky with so much growth around, and we don't want to miss where they may turn off."

Another hour of riding and they came to a little stream, on the banks of which was good grass. Slade decided the place was made to order for his purpose. He unsaddled and kindled a fire. He had come prepared for a night out or possibly two. From his saddle pouches he took a slab of bacon, a hunk of bread, and some eggs carefully wrapped against breakage, along with coffee, a little flat bucket and a small skillet, all an old campaigner needed to throw together a good meal. Soon coffee was bubbling in the bucket, bacon and eggs sizzling in the pan. After eating and smoking a cigarette, with the grass for a mattress, his single blanket for covering and his saddle for a pillow, he stretched out and was soon fast asleep.

With the first light he arose and cooked some breakfast. Full daybreak found him on his way again.

Before mid-morning, with the towering guardian walls of the pass, altitude three thousand feet, looming close, the trail turned sharply east and soon petered out in a welter of tall growth.

"In you go, feller," the Ranger said. "Other cayuses have gone through here, more than once, too. Look at those broken twigs and branches and the iron scratches on the stones."

Shadow went in, liking it not at all, but resignedly. For several hundred yards he forced his way through the tangle, until the chaparral thinned and the Comanche lay before them.

"Guessing right so far," Slade remarked as he turned his mount's nose north.

He rode warily through the pass but encountered no obstacle. Now his progress was slow, for here the tracks of the outlaw band were hard to follow and it would be easy to miss the point where they turned from the trail, as he was confident they would do. Some seven or eight miles north of the Gap, and about thirty miles south of Marathon, the tracks turned west into fairly thick growth. Soon they were following another of the old trails that resembled a snake path more than anything else.

Slade's caution increased, for he knew the outlaw hangout might not be far off and he had no desire to stumble on the bunch unawares. It would very likely be unhealthy to do so. Studying the ground over which he passed, he was of the opinion that the trail had been traveled by quite a few horses no very long time before. There were hoof marks coming and going, but it was impossible to ascertain in which direction they had passed last.

With startling abruptness the growth began to thin. Slade pulled Shadow to a slow walk and his vigilance increased. He strained his ears to catch the slightest sound, sniffed for traces of smoke. The silence remained unbroken, the air untainted.

"Just the same, feller, this is getting a bit hard on the nerves," he said. "I think you'd better hole up here for a spell and let me make the rest of the trip by way of shanks' mare. I don't kick up as much racket as you do. And for Pete's sake, don't go stomping your feet or singing songs."

Dismounting, he led the horse into the heart of a thicket some distance from the trail and left him there, confident that he would keep still. Then he returned to the track and stole ahead with the greatest caution, keeping close to the edge of the growth, ready to dive into it at the slightest alarm.

However, nothing happened. The silence remained unbroken save for the chirping of birds and the soft sighing of the wind in the leaves. The growth thinned still more. He reached a final straggle and a small clearing lay before him, across which ran a trickle of water.

And on the far side of the open space stood an old and weather-beaten but staunch-looking cabin such as was often come upon in this land of hunters, prospectors, and desert rats.

Very silent it stood. No smoke rose from its stick-and-mud chimney. Its door was shut and its single window was like a blank staring eye.

Over to one side and a little to the rear of the building was a lean-to for the accommodation of horses, much newer than the cabin. It was untenanted.

"Looks like nobody's home," Slade muttered. "But I'll bet a hatful of pesos this is it."

He hesitated at approaching the old shack. There was a chance that he could be mistaken, that horses not under the lean-to were off grazing somewhere, and occupants of the cabin asleep. However, reassured by the continuing silence, he took a chance and stole swiftly across the clearing.

At the closed door he paused, listening intently for any sound from within. The silence remained unbroken. He glanced around the clearing; it was empty, with no hint of movement anywhere in the surrounding brush. Reaching out, he gave the door a hard shove. It swung open on complaining hinges, and nothing happened. Cautiously he peered around the jamb for a quick look into the cabin. A single glance showed that there were no occupants within. Stepping in and closing the door behind him, he surveyed the single room. Very likely, years before, it had been the home of some wanderer of the hills, who had occupied it for a long time, perhaps had died here.

All around were signs of pioneer occupancy. There was a homemade table and chairs. In the wide fireplace were hooks for pots, an iron grill to accommodate skillets. A large Dutch oven stood nearby.

Also, there were plenty of signs of very recent occupancy by quite a few individuals. Bunks were built along the walls, with tumbled blankets on them. Several rifles of modern make stood in a corner. On shelves were stores of staple provisions. There was a bucket of water on a bench, still fresh.

In the ceiling was the opening of a trap door, and against a wall stood the homemade ladder by which it was reached. Here was undoubtedly the hole-up of a bunch, doubtlessly the outlaw band he sought.

Still studying the room, he pondered what to do with his discovery. The logical thing was to hole up in the brush and await developments. He had a feeling that the occupants of the cabin would return before long. They were due to, altogether too soon for Slade's liking.

Suddenly a sound broke the stillness, the sound of horses' hoofs thudding on the hard ground and voices speaking. Slade shot a glance out the window. Nearly a dozen horsemen were just emerging from the brush on the far side of the clearing and were heading straight for the cabin.

NINE

Slade glanced wildly about for a place of concealment; there was nothing in the room that would hide a healthy-sized rat. No back door, no back window. Then his glance fixed on the yawning opening of the trap door above his head. He started to fetch the ladder, but his mind was working at racing speed and instantly told him that moving it away from the wall might attract attention; somebody might recall it being placed there. Again he glanced up. The ceiling was comparatively low. He crouched, leaped upward, and caught the lip of the opening with one hand. A moment of furious struggle and he levered his body until his chest rested on the upper surface of the ceiling boards. Another instant of desperate effort and he was through the opening and rolled several feet away from it, just as the door opened and a number of men trooped in.

"Never mind the rigs, just fill their feed boxes and let them stand," a voice called, a voice with a familiar ring, the Ranger thought, of a peculiar bell-like quality once heard never forgotten.

Walt Slade knew he was in a very hot spot, trapped in the gloomy attic with a dozen killers in the room below. He glanced about, saw that there was a window minus sash and panes in the rear wall; but the opening was too small for him to slip through. On the floor nearby were sacks of grain, one of beans, another of coffee, still another of sugar. Also a couple of big lard cans, one empty. Evidently the attic was used as a storeroom for surplus supplies.

There were cracks between the floor boards, wide enough to give a view into the brighter room below. He peered through one and his breath caught in his throat.

A man was striding across the room to the fireplace, a man who walked with a panther-like tread. A very tall man, wide of shoulder, deep of chest, with a dark, handsome hawk-face and flashing black eyes.

"Veck Sosna himself!" El Halcón breathed. "I was right!"

Without a doubt it was the notorious Panhandle outlaw, the leader of the dread Comancheros, the man he sought. He'd found him at last. Fine! But Slade was not at all pleased with the manner in which he had found him. Right now the odds were distinctly in favor of Sosna.

Sosna spoke. "Mart," he said, "get a fire going and boil some coffee. When we leave, you can stay here and get ready to make us something to eat when we get back. The coffee will be plenty for now."

Slade held his breath, his eyes sliding toward the coffee sack. If Mart came up the ladder to fetch some, the fat was in the fire for fair. He let out his breath in a sigh of relief as one of the men took a covered can from a shelf and began spooning ground coffee into a big coffeepot.

Sosna drew a chair to the table and sat down, crossing his long legs. The others occupied the remaining chairs or the bunks. All rolled cigarettes and lit them. Slade noticed that today none had the dark dye smeared on their faces and hands; evidently they had given up the masquerade as no longer of use.

Slade felt that they would have looked better dyed, heavily dyed. He'd never seen a more villainous cast of countenances. Some, he was sure, had been members of Sosna's Comanchero band in north Texas; they all looked to have some Indian blood. The others, although pure white, were even worse in appearance. Sosna was speaking again.

"It oughtn't to take long to do the chore," he said. "That shebang runs on schedule and should be along in a couple of hours. After we have our coffee we'll slide down to the trail. No slip-ups this time, like with that infernal wagon train. Twenty thousand pesos will make a nice haul."

"You still figure it was El Halcón busted up the raid?" one of the men asked.

"Of course it was El Halcón, who else?" replied Sosna, his voice like steel grinding on ice, an expression of malignant hatred shadowing his face. "Wasn't he seen hobnobbing with the farmers at Morton? He rode with the train, of course. Nobody else would have figured things out like he did. Every time he shows up in a section there's trouble. This makes the third run-in I've had with him. He's the devil himself, always horning in on good things other people have lined up. He'll take those fool farmers for plenty before he's finished with them. What I'd like to know for sure is has he figured I'm here. I don't see how the devil he could, but there's no telling about the sidewinder. He's uncanny. I don't see how he could have trailed me to Mexico last year, but he did and busted up a good thing I had going. All I ask is a chance to get my hands on him alive; I'll see how long it'll take him to die, and before he does, he'll wish a thousand times he was dead."

He glared balefully about the room. Eyes shifted uneasily under his fell gaze. Veck Sosna ruled by terror. Silence followed for a while, then another of his followers ventured a question.

"Just where do you figure to pull it, Veck?" he asked.

"At the foot of that ridge a mile to the south of this track," Sosna replied. "There's scattered brush at its base, plenty to hide us from the trail, and close enough for good shooting. Shoot fast and shoot straight when I give the word; we're not taking any chances. Nobody to be left alive."

The others nodded their understanding, gloating expectation in their eyes.

Soon the coffee was bubbling. The man Mart broke out a number of tin cups, filled them and passed them around. The outlaws drank slowly, smoking between sips. Finally the empty cups clattered on the table. Sosna rose to his feet, towering over the others.

"All right, let's get going," he said. "Plenty of time, but we want to get all set. Mustn't take a chance on them being a bit early, which they could be. We'll be seeing you, Mart; we'll want to eat as soon as we get back, so have things in shape."

The outlaws trooped out. A moment later hoofs clicked away down the trail.

In the attic, Walt Slade was thinking furiously and in a fever of impatience. Somehow, he had to reach the Comanche in time to prevent whatever the devils had in mind, perhaps another wagon train to be burned and slaughtered. But how in blazes to get there with the man Mart in the room below! He hoped he'd place the ladder and come up for more provisions; but Mart showed no intention of doing so. Instead, he was puttering around the fireplace, which was at the side of the room farthest from the trap door. Slade contemplated leaning down and trying to disable him with a shot.

Quickly, however, he stifled the inclination; to make such a try at such an awkward angle would be quite likely just a good way to commit suicide. Something had to be done to attract Mart's attention away from the trap door, get him outside the cabin for a moment if possible, but what?

His gaze roamed over the shadowy attic, seeking vainly for some workable expedient, and found none. Escaping by way of the window was out of the question; it was altogether too narrow. And there was no other crack in the walls that would accommodate a skinny tomcat, much less his wide shoulders. The only means of exit was the trap door, which, with Mart in the room below, was no exit at all.

Again his eyes roved over his unpromising surroundings, fixed absently on the two lard cans, shifted to the narrow window, back to the cans, which were directly in line with where he lay and the window.

Suddenly he exclaimed under his breath. He

had it! Or believed he had. With the greatest care to make no sound, he crawled to one of the big cans, the empty one. It might work. Worth trying, anyhow. He didn't see how he could very well worsen his position. He got an arm around the can and carefully raised it from the floor. Now came the difficult part. Should he lose his grip on the slippery container, and in the awkward position of crawling with one hand, that would be easy to do, the jig would be up. Even a loudly creaking floor board might give him away. However, he took comfort in the fact that Mart was rattling pots and pans in the room below and making plenty of noise himself. Slowly, cautiously, he wormed his way toward the window. Once the racket in the room below abruptly ceased, as if Mart had heard something. But apparently he had only paused to roll and light a cigarette, for Slade caught a whiff of the tobacco smoke drifting through the cracks between the boards. The sound of his activities began again. Slade edged toward the window as fast as he dared.

After what seemed an eternity of straining effort, he reached it, awkwardly rose to his knees and peered out. There was nothing alive in sight. The ground below was hard and stony. He drew a deep breath, raised the can and dropped it out the window in a manner so it would bump against the wall as it fell.

The can behaved properly, it slammed against

the wall, hit the ground with a prodigious clang-jangle. In the room below, Mart uttered a startled exclamation. Slade heard Mart's boots thud across the room, heard the door banged open. He leaped to his feet, raced to the trap door and half dropped, half swung through the opening. He hit the floor with a thud, one boot heel slipped on a patch of grease and he fell heavily. Outside, Mart bellowed an oath. An instant later he loomed in the doorway, gun in hand.

Prone on the floor, Slade drew and shot from the hip. A bullet knocked splinters into his face. Another ripped through the crown of his hat. Then the outlaw reeled and fell, his chest riddled by the slugs from the Ranger's gun.

Slade scrambled to his feet, spared the dead man a single glance, then leaped over the body and sped to where he had left Shadow. Forking the black he sent him down the trail at a fast clip. He knew that if Sosna and his bunch paused for some reason, he might well barge into them around one of the sharp bends and find himself in an even hotter spot than the one he had occupied but a few minutes before. But he felt he had to take the chance if he was to hope to thwart whatever devilment they had in mind.

As he drew nearer the Comanche Trail, he slowed a bit, anxiously studying the terrain on his right, for he mustn't override where the ridge below the Comanche began. His instinct for distance and direction told him when he should turn off the track into the brush. It was hard going but Shadow negotiated it without the loss of too much hide. Finally he found himself behind the ridge, the upward slope of which was gentle. He sent Shadow diagonaling up the sag, slowing him more and more as he neared the crest, which was comparatively free of growth.

Finally he topped it, rode across its narrow level space, keeping in line with a stand of chaparral. On the far lip, screened by the brush, he pulled his mount to a halt and dismounted, sliding his Winchester from the boot. He wormed his way forward cautiously and quickly had a view of the Comanche below.

Almost instantly, he had a view of something else much more interesting. First he sighted the outlaws' horses, standing in a clump behind a thicket. Then he saw the men themselves, crouched less than fifty yards from the trail, peering to the north. They were some five hundred yards distant from where the Ranger stood.

And rolling down the Comanche, swiftly drawing near where the killers lurked in wait, was a big stagecoach drawn by eight horses. Slade could see a guard on the seat beside the driver. Another, rifle across his knees, sat in the boot behind.

TEN

The Marathon stage! Packing the twenty thousand dollars of which Sosna had spoken! Perhaps payroll money for the Terlingua quicksilver mines. Slade knew he had not a moment to spare if he was to save the lives of the driver and the guards. He flung the Winchester to his shoulder, his eyes glanced along the sights and he squeezed the trigger.

The report rang out like thunder. One of the outlaws reeled sideways and fell. Slade hoped it was Sosna, but the distance was too great to distinguish individuals in the shadow of the brush.

As the rifle spoke a second time, the outlaws whirled. Slade fired, again and again, as fast as he could pull trigger. Some wild shots echoed the reports, but the slugs did not come close.

A second man went down, kicking and writhing in his death agonies. The alert stage guards realized what was going on and began pouring bullets into the brush. A third dry-gulcher staggered but stayed on his feet. Caught between a deadly crossfire, the outlaws broke. There was a concerted rush for the horses. Swinging into their saddles, the killers raced northward, dodging in and out of the clumps of brush. Slade emptied the magazine of the repeater to speed them on their way. The stage guards kept blazing away with plenty of good intentions but no success. The fleeing outlaws dwindled away into the distance and vanished behind a belt of chaparral.

The guards and the driver were waving their hands to Slade. He waved back and sent Shadow down the slope, approaching the two bodies on the ground with caution. However, as he quickly saw, both had taken the Big Jump, and neither was Veck Sosna.

"I'm almost ready to believe the hellion does have a charmed life," he growled to Shadow. "He's boasted that the bullet was never run that could down him. Well, we'll see."

He paused long enough to give the bodies a once-over, discovering nothing of consequence; but he believed one, dark and hatchet-faced, had been a member of the Comanchero band of Panhandle outlaws. Looked like Sosna had collected the few left alive of his original Panhandle bunch and brought them with him.

"Would be just like him to go back to the Canadian River Valley country for them," Slade muttered. "The nerve of that sidewinder!"

When he rode out of the brush, the stage had pulled to a halt and the driver and the guards greeted him with enthusiasm.

"Don't know where you came from, cowboy, but you sure showed up at just the right time," the former shouted. "How come?"

"I was riding the crest of the ridge and spotted them holed up in the brush," Slade replied evasively. "Saw the stage approaching at about the same time, and it wasn't hard to figure what they had in mind. I decided they should be discouraged a mite."

"You discouraged them, all right," chuckled the driver. "Feller, I reckon me and Tom and Bob are sorta deep in your debt. If it hadn't been for you, we'd have been goners."

"Also, I suppose, the twenty thousand dollars you're packing along," Slade observed, trying a shot in the dark.

Both the driver and the guards looked decidedly startled.

"Nobody was supposed to know about that," the driver muttered.

"Well, it appears it was known by the wrong people," Slade remarked dryly. "Did any of you fellows happen to do some talking, say in a saloon or to a dance-floor girl?"

All three appeared thoroughly bewildered but shook their heads positively. "Ready to swear to it we didn't," one of the guards declared.

Slade nodded. Just another example of Sosna's uncanny ability to learn things he wasn't supposed to know.

"Payroll money was supposed to go on yesterday's coach," said the driver. "Strongbox was packed in, empty, for everybody to see. Then last night the real box containing the dinero was slipped into this coach."

Slade nodded again. An old expedient, supposed to throw possible raiders off the track. A trick that Sosna would see through instantly. The cunning devil, doubtlessly keeping a watch on the stage station, would instantly recognize the strategem and react accordingly. Which was exactly what he did.

"Well, guess we'd better be rolling," said the driver. He glanced apprehensively back along the trail.

"Figure there's any chance those hellions will come back and make another try?" he asked anxiously.

"I don't think so, but just the same I'll ride along with you for a spell, just in case, if you don't mind having me," Slade replied.

"We'll be darn glad to have you," declared the driver. "At Boraches Spring we pull aside and lay over at the Butterick ranch for the night. The company has an agreement with Butterick. You happen to know him?"

"I've met him," Slade replied noncommittally. "When you arrive at Terlingua, notify the authorities of what happened, so they can get in touch with the sheriff."

"We'll do that," the driver promised. "Okay? Let's go."

Slade was surprised at the warmth of John Butterick's greeting. And when the driver and the guards unfolded an account of the incident on the Comanche Trail, his enthusiasm knew no bounds.

"Felipe, my cook, was right on every count," he declared. "Yes, plumb right. And did you get your wagon train into Espantosa Valley? Tell me about it."

Slade told him, in detail, for he figured that a resident of the section should know. Butterick outdid his previous attempts at swearing.

"That blasted gang has got to be busted up," he declared. "And, son, I figure you're just the man to do it. Stick around with us and clean 'em. Yes, sir! El Halcón is the man for the chore!"

The eyes of the driver and guards widened. "El Halcón, the owlhoot!" Bob muttered.

Butterick turned on him with a roar of wrath. "Owlhoot!" he stormed. "He's about as much an owlhoot as you are. Maybe less so, for I've had an eye on you for quite a spell. Wouldn't be a bit surprised if it was you, blabbermouth, who let it out that the Terlingua payroll money was on the stage. Shut up before I bust you one, even if you are in my house, you terrapin-brained frazzle end of a misspent life!"

"Blazes! Mr. Butterick, I didn't mean anything," stammered the disconcerted guard. "I just repeated what a lot of folks have said."

"Uh-huh, a lot more terrapin-brains like yourself," growled Butterick. "All right, all right, forget it. Let's go eat."

Slade, his eyes mirthful, winked at the discomfited Bob, and they repaired to the dining room.

The stage resumed its journey at daybreak. Slade accompanied it to where the old track leading to Espantosa Valley joined the Comanche.

"You should be okay from here on," he told the driver. "Be seeing you."

"And much obliged again, feller, for everything," the driver replied. The guards added their thanks. Slade waved his hand and turned Shadow's nose west.

When he reached the valley, Slade was quite surprised at the progress the farmers had made during the short period of his absence.

"Everything going fine," Worthington told him. "This brush isn't hard to clear—I've tackled a lot worse."

"Fortunately it's not mesquite," Slade observed. "That has a tremendous root system; main roots are sometimes forty feet long, and they go deep. Like all true desert plants, it must have an extensive spread of roots to survive. In no other way could it draw enough water to flourish."

"Timber on the slopes is fine, too," Worthington added. "We'll be housed proper before cold weather sets in. This soil is going to grow fine crops, and we hope to bring in some cattle, too, once the grass gets going good. Oh, we're plumb satisfied with what you led us to, and we'll never forget it. Now you'd better go look up Leela— she's been worried about you. She's at her wagon down there. Old Lije has been worried, too. Said you should have taken him with you."

"He's a good man to have along on an expedition," Slade conceded. "However, there are times when I'm better off by myself. This one, for instance."

"Run up against something?" Worthington asked curiously. Slade gave an account of his adventures. The farmer shook his head and swore.

"Anyhow," he commented hopefully, "you're thinning 'em out. Yep, you sure are. I've done lost count of how many."

"But the head of the outfit is still going strong," Slade said. "So long as he's running around loose there'll continue to be trouble. I've learned from experience how quickly he can get another bunch together. He's a born leader and the sort that attracts the orneriest and most ruthless. Well, maybe his luck will run out sometime."

"It will," Worthington predicted confidently.

"I've a notion Lije is correct when he maintains that right always comes out on top, sooner or later."

"Here's hoping," Slade agreed cheerfully, and went in search of Leela.

He found her in her wagon, watching the progress of the small house that was being built for her. She gave a glad little cry and clung to him for a moment.

"I was worried, terribly worried," she confessed. "And—and—"

"Yes?" he prompted.

"And—lonely."

"Even with the stars for company?"

"Yes, darn it, even with the stars. I tried them, but they were cold comfort. The darn things seemed to be laughing at me. I guess the stars aren't enough for a girl."

"Well," he smiled, "they do look better with company. They'll be shining tonight."

"Yes," she said, very softly, and blushing.

Old Lije Crane's greeting was also warm. "Knew darn well you'd be getting into trouble if you were out of my sight," he declared. "See what you're doing to me? Next thing I'll be really swearing. Tell us what you've been up to."

Slade told them, precisely, for he was anxious that the farmers not be lulled into a sense of false security.

By the time he had finished, Leela was

shuddering, and old Lije was really very close to wholehearted profanity.

"The dirty scuts!" he growled. "I sure wish I'd been with you. Maybe we'll get another crack at them," he added hopefully.

"Not beyond the realm of possibility," Slade conceded. "There'll never be any peace until they are thoroughly cleaned out."

"Just a matter of time," said Lije. "Just a matter of time. That sort isn't allowed to clutter up the earth forever. Yep, just a matter of time."

Slade hoped that Lije Crane would prove to be a prophet with honor in his own country.

The valley was a hive of industry. Everywhere, walls were rising. Trees were felled on the slopes, the branches trimmed away, the logs snaked down by horse-power. Later, when title was gotten and the land duly apportioned, individual farmhouses would rise; but now the community was laid out as a tight village.

"Next spring we'll plant a community crop," Worthington explained. "That'll give us a start. Later, it'll be every man for himself.

"I think," he added, a contemplative light in his eyes, "that before long I'll make a little trip to Morton and grab off that gal I told you about. Hope she'll still be waiting for me."

"I'm very much of the opinion she will be," Slade replied smilingly. "I don't think you have anything to worry about on that score. Struck me as the right sort and will make a good farmer's wife."

"I hope so," Worthington replied. "I've been sorta lonely since my first wife died. As the Bible says, it's not good for a man to live alone."

"And that also applies to a woman," Slade said.

"You're sort of alone," Worthington commented. "Got a notion it would be good for you to settle down with—with somebody nice."

"Perhaps," Slade conceded. But just the same, as he spoke, his eyes were fixed on the mountain tops to the south.

ELEVEN

The farmers had brought a good deal of furniture with them; but more was needed and preparations were being made to provide it. The boards for a homemade table would be shaved with a drawknife. Stools and benches would be constructed from the lumber of a split tree and faced with a broadax. Bedsteads would be mortised into the walls and strung with rawhide ropes for the mattress. Some had brought stoves; other would depend on wide fireplaces equipped with hooks for pots and kettles. There would be either a grill in the fireplace for the accommodation of pans, or three-legged skillets resting over the coals. The floors of the cabins would be puncheons—split poles—the door, of clapboards hewn from logs. The fireplace would be backed with stone. An ambitious chimney would be of stone. One less pretentious of mud and sticks.

When the supply of candles and oil for lanterns were exhausted, candles would be made by pouring warm tallow into a mold. If one wasn't handy, strings would be dipped into warm tallow, the process repeated as the tallow hardened, until the proper thickness was achieved.

These hardy pioneers would make nature serve them in a multitude of ways and in consequence would lack for nothing needed to provide rude comfort, even luxury. Walt Slade thought it a great privilege to be able to lend such folks a helping hand. It was such things that made Ranger work really worth-while and accounted for the fascination it held for him.

Seating himself comfortably on a wagon tongue, he rolled and lit a cigarette and reviewed recent events, with the purpose of ascertaining what capital could be made from them. One thing appeared obvious: Sosna, or some of his men, spent time in Marathon. Otherwise the outlaw leader would hardly have been able to learn that the stage packed the Terlingua payroll money for which he made the try. That, Slade felt, might work to his advantage.

He pondered the cabin hangout in the woods.

Should he notify the sheriff of the county of its existence and have him keep an eye on it? After due consideration he dismissed the idea. Sosna would never use the cabin again after he found the body of his henchman beside the door. His keen mind would at once conclude that El Halcón had nosed out his hole-up. And, Slade believed, he quite likely had another place of refuge somewhere between Marathon and Morton. Like a fox, he always had more than one burrow to his earth.

After his recent setback, and knowing that El Halcón was on his trail, it was unlikely that he would attempt another raid on the farmers; but the possibility could not be fully dismissed. Sosna was noted for doing the unexpected. No angle could be ignored where the cunning devil was concerned.

He began recounting Sosna's recent losses. Not more than twenty had taken part in the raid on the wagon train. Of these, nine were dead. One had died in the cabin hideout, two in the brush beside the Comanche trail. So unless Sosna had a reserve stashed away somewhere, his band now numbered, including himself, not more than eight. Which was a rather small force to hope to stage an effective attack on the farmers. Which, he felt, made the situation not too bad. However, as long as Veck Sosna was running around loose, there was still plenty to worry about. Slade pondered what his next move would be, and for the time being was unable to reach a decision. He pinched out his cigarette butt and went to confer with Van Worthington.

"Yes, I've kept the guards posted, day and night," Worthington replied to his question. "So far they haven't spotted anything off-color. But we figure to take no chances till you tell us the coast is clear."

"The sensible thing to do," Slade commented. "I'm inclined to believe you won't need to worry about another raid, but you can't be sure. Better to be safe than sorry."

Worthington was glad of a chance to rest his back and stretch his legs for a brief period, so they walked about as they talked. They paused near a boy who was industriously scraping a green hide. Worthington chuckled.

"There's a blacksmith shop, a cobbler's, a saddler's, a tailor's, and a carpenter's all rolled up in one," he observed. "From it you can make ropes, clotheslines, bedsprings, seats for chairs, an overcoat, britches, or a pair of brogans, and a shirt. You can tie up a loose tire with strips, or the busted pieces of a wagon. Tie king posts and rafters with it and when it dries it tightens and gets hard as iron; will last you forever."

Slade nodded his understanding. All these people asked was a chance to make much from little. He grimly determined they would get it.

With no plan as yet for his campaign against Sosna, Slade spent the following day exploring the valley more fully. A number of springs gushed from beneath the east slopes, each forming its own little brook to meander across the level ground to the west wall where, sooner or later, it dived into some crevice.

On the banks of the streams, grass grew luxuriantly, providing ample forage for the horses. Needle and wheat grass predominated, excellent for cattle.

"Yes, later, if you take a notion, you can run in cows," he told Worthington. "They'd thrive here, for once the brush is cleared away the grass will grow like blazes. I figure you'll have enough spare land after your planting to accommodate quite a herd. Keep it in mind. Then your own meat supply will be cared for and you'll have a surplus to dispose of at a nice profit."

"We'll do it," replied Worthington. "We'll buy cows as soon as we are in a position to handle them. We're not exactly poverty-stricken; quite a bit of money in the bank back in Kentucky. We arranged a community fund in my name before we left, to take care of buying land, and so forth. Didn't put out anything much in the Nueces country, so we're in pretty good shape."

"That's fine," Slade said, "and while we're discussing the matter, I'd advise you to get title to your holding here without delay. I'll make a cadastral survey, after a fashion. I can approximate distances well enough to get by. They won't be overly particular about a section here and it won't cost you a great deal. Very little, in fact. The government is glad to get settlers in this part of the state. I'll write a letter that will take care of the details.

"And," he added, "I think it would be a good idea for you and me to ride to Marathon, the railroad town, get in touch with the Land Office and close the deal. How about day after tomorrow?"

"Fine!" answered Worthington. "And it's sure mighty nice of you to lend a hand this way; it'll be a big help."

"I was planning a trip to Marathon in the next day or two, anyhow, so I won't be going out of my way," Slade said.

"I've a notion the Reverend will want to go along," Worthington remarked. "He doesn't seem to like you out of his sight."

"That's okay," Slade replied. "He's a good man to have along."

Old Lije did want to go along and stated definitely that he was going along. That was all right with Slade; but from another quarter came a declaration equally definite of which he was a trifle dubious.

"I'm going, too," Leela declared flatly. "I want to make some purchases in town."

120

"You'll have to sleep under the stars at night," Slade teased, when they were alone. "It's a two-day ride."

Miss Austin tossed her unruly curls. "Be the same stars, won't they?" she replied, pointedly.

Slade was not at all averse to having her company on the trip but, conditions being what they were, he experienced a moment of disquietude. However, it was unlikely that anything untoward would occur, so he offered no objections.

The trip to Marathon was without incident, and the stars accommodatingly refrained from veiling their faces in clouds. Arriving at the town, as the first order of business, Slade exchanged several telegrams with the Land Office, and sent one to another "office" in the capital. As a result, he finally told Worthington, "All set to go. You can fill out your check—here's the amount—and send it along with the other papers."

Worthington shook his head in bewilderment. "Never saw a thing go through so smooth and fast," he declared. "You must know somebody over there."

Slade smiled but refrained from further comment.

"Now I'll meet Leela at the general store across the street, as I promised to," he said. "I've a notion she can find everything she wants there, for this town is the supply center for the ranching country that extends almost across the six thousand square miles of Brewster County, which is larger than quite a few eastern states."

"Hard to get used to the distances here," sighed Worthington. "Seems like there's no end to this darn state."

"Well, you can ride a day and a night on a railroad train and still be in Texas," Slade replied. "Yep, she's a pretty good-sized chunk of territory."

Slade found Leela in the store, making certain purchases that were beyond masculine comprehension. So he found a place to sit down and smoked in comfort until she had finished the chore.

"I'm hungry," she announced, after she had loaded him with packages. "No wonder! It's getting dark."

"We should have brought along a pack mule," he groaned, clutching at a slippery bundle.

"Oh, most of them will go in the saddle pouches," she replied cheerfully. "I want to eat."

"All right, as soon as we dump these in your hotel room," he agreed. "I know a saloon that puts out about the best chuck in town. I told Van and Lije we would meet them there."

The saloon in question was typical cow country and Slade paid it little mind. But it was novel enough to Leela to arouse her interest. She eyed with approval the dance-floor girls in their spangled short skirts and low-cut bodices.

"Can anybody dance?" she asked. "I like to dance."

"Of course," he replied. "Fact is, I wouldn't be surprised if you could get a job of dancing here, if you took a notion to."

"I think I'd like it," she said. "The place is really interesting."

"Too darn interesting at times, I've a notion," he answered, glancing at the young cowhands lining the bar.

Leela did not appear unduly impressed by the remark. "After we finish eating, we'll dance, if you don't mind," she said.

"I like to dance, too," he admitted. "So does Van, and he dances well; I watched him in Morton. I suppose you frown on such frivolous activities, eh, Reverend?"

Old Lije shook his head. "I can shake a hoof a mite myself," he replied. "Our church does not disapprove of dancing or any other harmless entertainment. After all, our Lord changed the water into wine at the wedding feast, so folks could enjoy themselves. He was not averse to folks having a good time."

"Otherwise, He would hardly have made the world so beautiful," Slade said gently. Old Lije bowed his head in silent agreement.

Slade could not but be impressed by the

change a few short weeks had wrought in the old gentleman. He was something quite different from the austere, bigoted individual he was when they first met. Well, this land of great distances and rugged grandeur was bound to have its effect on the mind of anyone who could think, and Elijah Crane was not lacking in intelligence. It was hard to be repressed and self-centered amid so much magnificence.

He was not enough of an egoist to reflect that the gentle, persistent pressure of his own personality had much to do with the change in Elijah Crane.

TWELVE

The place was filling up and rapidly becoming more boisterous. Song, of a sort, blended with the music of the very good orchestra. Sometimes the blend was not exactly ninety-proof, but nobody seemed to mind.

"I've a notion it's payday for a number of the neighborhood spreads," Slade remarked. "Sure looks that way. Well, it makes for a lively night."

The noisy and hilarious atmosphere appeared to have an exhilarating effect on Leela. Her eyes sparkled, her cheeks were flushed. Plenty of glances were cast in her direction. Those directed at Slade were slightly tinged with good-natured envy. More so when after they had finished eating, she and Slade invaded the dance floor and showed the onlookers what really good dancing could be like.

"You're a wonderful partner," Leela exclaimed breathlessly after they finished the first lively number.

"You're not bad yourself when it comes to dancing," he replied.

She dimpled up at him. "Is that all?" she asked softly.

"Well," he smiled, "we'll just say you're a wonderful partner."

"That's better," she said. "Listen, they're starting a waltz; I love waltzes; they're so dreamy."

"And you're satisfied with dreams?"

"I have to be, as you very well know," she replied simply.

"I can't help the way I'm made," he said.

"I try to make allowances for that," she answered. "I know for you no woman has the allure to equal what's over the next hilltop. Nice to have you while you are around, though. Let's dance!"

They danced several more numbers, then Leela said she was tired.

"I'm going to bed," she announced. "I suppose you'll be staying up till all hours."

"I do want to look around a bit," he admitted.

"Try and keep out of trouble for a change," she begged.

"I will," he promised. He walked her to the hotel and then returned to the saloon, where Worthington and old Lije appeared to be thoroughly enjoying themselves.

"Good to have a chance to relax a bit," said the former.

Slade thought so, too, and welcomed a bit of diversion after the recent hectic days and weeks. Although very much on the lookout for anything off-color, he resolved to take it easy if possible and not bother his head over anything.

However, as the hours passed, he began to experience a vague but uneasy premonition that something untoward was happening or going to happen soon. He tried to shake it off, but it persisted, intruding on his thoughts, like a thin mist creeping between tree branches, vague, impalpable, illusory, but very real. He had experienced such presentiments before and had learned not to ignore them. And with Veck Sosna loose in the section, anything could happen and probably would.

His gaze was constantly on the swinging doors, when it was not roving about the crowded room, studying every man who came or went. So far, however, he had not noted anybody calculated to arouse his suspicions. Of course, most any member of Sosna's bunch could enter without attracting any particular attention. For, so far as Slade knew, none of them had anything like the striking appearance of the outlaw chieftain. In any gathering, Veck Sosna stood out, stood out like a stalking panther in the company of cheerfully truculent wolves. Slade knew that did the Panhandle owlhoot step in the door he would instantly recognize him, but he had not the least notion that Sosna would appear; he was far too shrewd for that. Before he entered a place, Sosna was sure as to who would be present, and there was little doubt but that he was on the constant lookout for El Halcón.

So blast it! What was bothering him? He couldn't for the life of him put a finger on it; but it was there, and insisting on attention.

Could Walt Slade have been fifteen or sixteen miles to the west of Marathon at the moment, he would have realized that his premonition of trouble in the making was soundly founded.

The *Western Flyer* was late, and old Cal Pender, the engineer, was doing his best to make up time. Bouncing about on the lurching seat box in the cab of the great locomotive, he peered ahead, estimated his speed, hooked the reverse lever up a couple more notches, widened the throttle a little more. The thundering exhaust quickened. The clanging side-rods were a steely blur, the huge main-rods a rhythmic flash, up and down, back and forth in unison with the spinning wheels. The tires screamed shrill protest as they ground against the bent rails of a curve. The headlight beam bored into the star-burned darkness, cutting a clean swath through the clustering shadows, glinting on the trunks of trees, silvering the twigs, beating back from massive boulders that lined the right-of-way. Like a comet on the loose, the *Western Flyer* roared through the night, its long line of coaches rocking and swaying, their lighted windows rectangles of ruddy gold.

Joe Grace, the fireman, glanced at the steam gauge needle quivering against the two-hundred-pound pressure peg, peered across at the water gauge. Both injectors were wide open, pouring streams of water into the straining boiler. He leaped to the deck, swung open the firebox door. A hot glare filled the cab, and the musical clang of a shovel as he gave the "hog" a good feed of coal. He scrambled back onto the seat box as the locomotive lurched at the beginning of a sweeping curve, the inner arc on his side. He peered out the window and gave a yell: "Look out, Cal, look out! There's something burning ahead—looks like it's the ties!"

Old Cal slammed the throttle shut, grabbed the automatic brake handle. The shoes screamed against the tires; air whistled through the port. The long train leaped and bucked.

From directly ahead came a sullen boom and a

blinding flash, through which cascaded splintered ties and earth and stones. The engine, its speed little abated, roared toward the smoking crater beneath the sagging rails. It struck the gaping hole, reeled, and overturned on its side. Joe Grace was pinned between the crushed side of the cab and the hot iron of the boiler. His screams of agony rent the air, died to sobbing moans, stilled.

The express car teetered and tottered on the edge of the excavation the dynamite had hollowed out, but it stayed on the rails. Old Cal, bruised and bleeding, crawled from the wrecked cab as a group of men bulged from the nearby brush, guns blazing. He fell dead without a groan. A moment later a brakeman who had dropped from the front of the foremost coach also fell. The cries of injured and frightened passengers arose as bullets slammed through the windows.

A stick of dynamite, its short-cut fuse trailing sparks and smoke, soared through the air. It exploded as it struck the baggage-car door, blowing it to pieces.

Two men rushed forward and clambered through the opening. More shots sounded, and a shriek of pain. One of the men, tall, flashing-eyed, stepped over the body of the slain express messenger and knelt beside the big iron safe. Ear pressed to the door, he deftly twirled the combination knob. Outside, the other raiders kept on shooting at the coaches to discourage interference.

Very quickly, the man by the safe uttered a satisfied exclamation, swung open the ponderous door and began tossing out canvas sacks, some of which rustled, others clinking musically. His companion gathered them into his arms. The pair leaped from the car, were joined by the others and rushed back into the brush. The click of fast hoofs sounded, fading into the distance. The whole grisly episode had taken little more than five minutes.

THIRTEEN

The Marathon saloon, despite the lateness of the hour, was still noisy and gay. Slade and his companions sat at their table, cups of coffee before them, and talked.

Suddenly a wildly excited man rushed in. "Boys," he shouted, "it just came over the wire— some hellions wrecked the *Western Flyer*, killed about half the crew and the express messenger and busted open the express car safe! Don't know how much they got, but I betcha it was plenty. The conductor cut in on the wire and called for help. They're sending the wreck train and trying to get hold of the sheriff. A lot of good he can do! The devils sashayed into the brush and will be in

Mexico or some place before he catches up with 'em."

Amid the bellowing of questions and answers, Walt Slade stood up. With unhurried steps he walked to the informant, Worthington and old Lije trailing behind. He took the excited man by the shoulder and twisted him around.

"Just where did it happen?" he asked quietly. The man, the Ranger's steady eyes hard on his face, answered without hesitation: "Between here and Alpine, nearly twenty miles to the west, I gather, this side of Dugout Mountain." Slade nodded and turned to his companions.

"I'm riding over there," he announced.

"And we'll ride with you," Worthington instantly replied.

"Okay," Slade said, "but we'll be riding fast." He took a notebook and a pencil from his pocket, scribbled a few words and tore out the sheet.

"Van, give this to the desk clerk at the hotel and tell him to be sure Leela gets it in the morning," he directed. "I'm telling her to wait here in town until we get back. We'll probably be gone all day and part of tomorrow night. Go ahead, I'll get the rig on your horse."

They did ride fast, but dawn was flushing the eastern sky with rose and gold when they arrived at the scene of the wreck. The wreck train had arrived and workmen were repairing the track so that the train, with a fresh engine, could continue on its way. A spur was being built onto which the wreck train would be shunted to clear the way for the *Flyer.* Passengers stood around in groups, some injured, though none seriously. Slade approached the conductor, who was standing nearby.

"Sheriff arrived yet?" he asked. The conductor shook his head.

"Understand he was out somewhere; don't know when he got the word. Reckon he'll be along soon, though."

The fireman's crushed and burned body had been retrieved and was laid out beside those of the brakeman, the engineer, and the express messenger. Slade gazed down at the still forms, and his eyes were terrible.

"Yes, Sosna and his bunch of devils again," he told Worthington. "Well, maybe this will be his finish. Blazes, I wish the sheriff would get here!"

However, the morning was well along before Sheriff Cain Dobson put in a tardy appearance, a posse of half a dozen men at his heels. He spotted the tall Ranger instantly, swung from the saddle and strode forward.

"Slade!" he exclaimed. "Where in tarnation did you come from? Feller, am I glad to see you! This is hell, and I've not the least notion where those sidewinders headed for."

"I think I know," Slade replied. "Let your

horses rest a bit and we'll hightail. Be an all-day ride, though."

"I don't care if it takes a month, just so we catch up with those snake-blooded blankety blanks!" the sheriff swore.

It was an all-day ride to where the hidden trail led to the outlaw hangout, although they saved a few miles by way of a shortcut that bypassed Marathon. Slade did not push the horses, not knowing how badly they might need them later.

"We've either got plenty of time or none at all," he told Sheriff Dobson. "If they headed for where I think they did, they'll spend the night there. If they didn't, the devil alone knows where they went, and he won't tell. So we can take it easy, even stop for something to eat—I suppose you brought provisions along in your pouches? Wouldn't be like you not to."

"We did," replied the sheriff. "Didn't know how long we might be out. I made up my mind to run those hellions down if I had to follow them clean to the other end of Mexico, international law be damned! Yep, we've got enough along to feed a regiment. And right now it's way past noon and I'm hungry. We'll stop at the next spring or crik. Okay?"

"Okay by me," Slade agreed, for if he was right in his hunch, there really was no need to hurry.

He really was following a hunch, one based on his knowledge of Veck Sosna and how his mind worked. He believed that Sosna would reason that El Halcón would reason that he, Sosna, would not return to the cabin after finding his dead follower by the cabin door. Which was just what Slade did, in the beginning. But he and the outlaw leader had been matching wits for quite a while. So much so that each had a fair inkling as to just how the other's thought processes operated. So Slade figured he was thinking a bit ahead of Sosna in believing now that he would return to the cabin after his successful raid on the *Western Flyer*. If he was wrong, there wasn't much of anything lost. If he was right, well, it might be the finish of the pest for good and all. That is if Sosna didn't do some thinking of his own that would put him ahead of the Ranger. That had to be taken into consideration, which Slade did not lose sight of for a moment.

It was almost full dark when they reached the spot where the old trail began. Slade recalled that on his previous ride he had noted a stand of sotol nearby. So he directed that an armload of dry stalks be broken off and packed along against the possibility that torches might come in handy. Later he was to be devoutly thankful for taking that precaution.

They entered the trail and rode slowly and

cautiously, peering and listening. However, the track ran on and on, deserted. No sound broke the silence save the small sounds of their going. Everything seemed utterly peaceful.

But as they progressed, Slade again experienced disquietude and apprehension. So strong did the premonition of trouble ahead grow that when they were something less than a mile from the clearing he abruptly called a halt.

"Cain," he said to the sheriff, "I don't like it. I've a feeling that I've been outsmarted, that if we ride up to the front of that cabin we're going to barge into something. If the hellions have guessed what we plan to do and are holed up waiting for us, we wouldn't have a show. It'll be tough going, but I figure we'd better circle through the brush and approach the cabin from the rear. Yes, it will be tough going, but our lives may well depend on it."

"I sure won't argue the point," replied Dodson. "If you figure that's the right thing to do, that's what we'll do. You've had a mite more experience at this sort of thing than any of the rest of us. What do you think, boys?"

There was general agreement.

"Never knew him to be wrong," declared Van Worthington.

It *was* tough going, and both men and horses lost some hide in the process; but after a long and miserable period of fighting the thorny brush,

Slade announced that they should be in line with the rear of the cabin and less than a quarter of a mile from it.

"I think we'd better leave the horses here with one man to watch them," he decided. "Then if one of them takes a notion to sing a song, it will do no harm. Best not to take chances. Bring those sotol stalks along."

With the greatest caution they stole through the brush on foot, pausing often to listen for sounds of life ahead. The silence remained unbroken and nowhere was there any sign of movement. Finally through a last straggle of growth, they sighted the cabin. To all appearances it was deserted. No light shone through the chinks in the log walls. Slade could see there were no horses in the lean-to.

"I don't believe there's anybody in there," breathed Dobson.

"Wait," Slade whispered reply. He was studying the top of the stick and mud chimney.

Suddenly he saw it—a thin trickle of smoke misting against the stars.

"They're in there, or have been," he told Dobson. "There's been a fire going; it's almost died out, but is still sending off a bit of smoke. Now what the devil are we to do? There's no rear door to that shack, and we don't dare chance slipping around to the front. Wait, this will take some thinking out."

For some moments he stood silent, gazing at the shadowy loom of the building.

"I believe I've got it," he whispered. "Lije, you slip back to the horses—I know you can go quietly—and fetch my rope."

Crane nodded and slid away silently as a wraith. Slade groped about on the ground and finally came up with a fair-sized and rough boulder. When Crane returned with the sixty-foot sisal, he tied one end securely to the stone and several of the dry sotol stalks.

"Now," he told his followers, "divide up and slide out to the side, so that you'll have a view of anybody coming out the front of the shack. I think I can bring them out. As soon as they show, let them have it. You are in charge, Cain, as the peace officer. You can give them a chance to surrender if you wish; it's up to you."

"Lots of chance they gave those poor devils on that train," was the sheriff's only response.

Slade waited until he was sure all were in position. Then he edged forward out of the growth and wrapped the free end of the rope about his left arm, making sure that it was securely fastened. He gauged the distance to the cabin, the building's width.

"Sixty foot should do it and to spare," he muttered. He fumbled a match from his pocket, struck it on the stone and touched the tiny flicker to the sotol, which instantly burned with a clear, bright flame. Stepping forward, he hurled the stone and the blazing stalks. The missile soared over the cabin roof, the rope trailing behind. The rope tightened and Slade heard the resounding thump as the stone banged against the front wall of the cabin. The ridge of the roof stood out clear in the glare of burning sotol. He frantically jiggled the rope; the stone banged and hammered against the wall.

From inside the cabin came a muffled yell, and another, and a torrent of curses. He heard the front door bang open; the cursing grew louder, was drowned in a bellow of gunfire. The sheriff's voice soared above the uproar: "Let 'em have it, boys, let 'em have it! Don't let one of the blankety-blank-blanks get away!"

Slade held onto the rope for another moment; for the glare of the burning sotol would outline the owlhoots, while the posse were in the shadow. Then, as quickly as he could, he disengaged his arm and raced to join the sheriff.

But before he reached him, he heard another sound, a sound that brought an exasperated oath to his lips—the sound of fast hoofs drumming away from the clearing. Some of the hellions were escaping; must have had the horses ready for a quick get-away should one be in order. Again Sosna's absolutely uncanny genius for overlooking no slightest detail!

FOURTEEN

The firing had ceased when Slade reached the sheriff's side. "Yes, a couple of 'em got away," said Dobson. "I figure we did for the rest of them—bodies scattered all around. Let's make sure, though."

They approached the bodies and the cabin warily, but there was no need for caution. Seven dead men lay in the clearing; there was nobody in the building.

By the light of a torch, Slade hopefully examined the bodies. He was doomed to disappointment, though; Veck Sosna was not among them.

"Always in the clear," he growled. "He's the limit! If I could have brought Shadow with me instead of leaving him a quarter of a mile back in the brush, I might have run down the hellion."

"Would have been too risky," the sheriff consoled. "No horse could have come through that brush without kicking up a racket; it would have given the whole thing away and very likely it would be us with our toes up instead of them."

"I suppose so," Slade conceded morosely.

A whoop sounded from inside the cabin. "Slade, Sheriff, come here and see what we've found," called Van Worthington's voice.

They hurried into the shack. Worthington was waving a torch and pointing to one of the bunks. On it lay a heap of canvas sacks.

"The money!" exclaimed the sheriff. "They didn't take time to divide it. Walt, your hunch was sure plumb correct. They figured we'd come here looking for them and were all set. Figured, too, that we'd be right on their tail and they didn't have any time to waste. They got the early start, but they had the longest way to go and had to circle through the brush; wouldn't have taken a chance on the Comanche."

"Right, I guess," Slade agreed. "Well, that helps some. For once Sosna slipped a mite— didn't have the best part of it stashed in his saddle pouches."

"Taken all around, a darn good night's work," chuckled Dobson. "Well, I'm hungry again and there 'pears to be plenty of good chuck in here. Suppose we make some coffee and cook us a bite."

Nobody offered any objections. Old Lije insisted on taking over the cooking chore and before long they sat down to a good meal, their appetites not in the least impaired by the carcasses lying just outside the door.

"Pitching that rock and the sotol over the roof was just about the smartest trick I ever heard tell of," chuckled the sheriff. "Yes, sir, it was a lulu! Reckon the horned toads thought the shack was caving in, or something. And when they ran out, the fire blinded them and they couldn't see to shoot, while we had all the good shooting light we needed. I felt the wind of a coupla slugs, but nobody even got nicked. Which was a lot better than I'd hoped for. A plumb smart trick!"

The others chimed in their chorus of admiration.

"Well, something had to be done," Slade smiled.

"It was plenty," said Dobson. "Well, the horses are all cared for, but they'll need a mite of rest, so I reckon we might as well try and knock off a little shut-eye ourselves. Good broncs those hellions were riding; I couldn't place the brands."

"Two of them were Panhandle bums," Slade said. "I'm not sure about the others."

"We'll use 'em to pack the carcasses to town and lay 'em out for folks to look over," said the sheriff. "And you figure one of the devils that got away was really Sosna?"

"Absolutely," Slade replied. "He wrecked and robbed a train up in the Panhandle with precisely the same method. He's utterly callous and ruthless. The fact that fifty passengers might have been killed had that train turned over meant nothing to him. He takes a sadistic pleasure from torturing and killing. Snake-blooded, cruel, and smart. An educated man. Studied medicine and I expect he is as good a doctor as he is a safe-cracker. Graduated from a university, *summa cum laude*, and has a Ph.D. degree. A mad genius gone wrong. Regrettable; in any line of honest endeavor he would have made his mark, but somewhere, somehow he took the wrong fork of the trail. As I remarked once before, sometimes I think he isn't a man but a devil. And he sure seems to always get the breaks."

"Anyhow, it looks like we pretty well busted up his gang," said Dobson.

"Yes, but his sort quickly gets another together," Slade replied. "And after this setback, he'll be doubly dangerous. Well, we'll see."

The sheriff nodded to a heap in a corner. "Over there's what we took off the hellions," he remarked. "Thought maybe you might want to look it over. What shall we do with the dinero they were packing? Quite a bit of it."

"Might be a good idea to use it to start a fund for the families of those trainmen who were killed," Slade suggested.

"That's a notion," agreed the sheriff. "We'll do it."

Before joining the others in rest, Slade rummaged through the heap of odds and ends, and discovered nothing he considered of significance.

Not that he was surprised at his lack of success. Veck Sosna did not hand out written instructions, or allow anything to be kept that might provide a clue to his whereabouts. He told his followers what to do, verbally, in his bell-like voice, and they did it, or else.

At daybreak the company was astir. Old Lije cooked a hearty breakfast and after eating they were ready to start.

"We'll lay over in Marathon tonight," the sheriff decided. "Forty miles and better is enough for one day's jaunt with led pack horses. All set? Let's go."

Sheriff Dobson and the others were highly elated over the success of the expedition and chattered gaily as they rode. Slade, on the other hand, was mostly silent. For he still had a real problem to face. Where the devil would Sosna head for, and where would he bust loose next? His activities might be curtailed for a while, but not for long. The resourceful hellion would soon recover from his setback and be on the prod again. He wouldn't take kindly to being outsmarted and would be bent on evening up the score. Slade's hope was for an opportunity to come to grips personally with the outlaw. So far it had been like doing battle with a shadow, a very solid and substantial shadow, but nevertheless a shadow so far as real contact was concerned.

He tried, as often before, to put himself

in Sosna's position—fleeing, his outfit of desperadoes smashed, with, so far as Slade knew, only one follower left. But Veck Sosna was a host unto himself. Also, he might well have a reserve somewhere. Perhaps at or around Morton, to the east. If so, it was logical that he would endeavor to join them and start operations anew. In the vast Trans-Pecos and Big Bend country there were always opportunities for the enterprising outlaw. If there were not, Sosna would make them. His harassing of the wagon trains was an example of his genius for ferreting out lucrative depredations.

Yes, Sosna was at the moment very likely planning some fresh atrocity. It was up to him, Slade, to, if possible, forestall it.

The entry into Marathon was something in the nature of a triumphal procession; it appeared everybody was on the street. Sheriff Dobson had a branch office in the cow-town and there the bodies were laid out for inspection. People crowded in to view them. Controversial discussions raged. Some were positive that they had seen one or more of the miscreants in town; but nobody could advance anything definite relative to them or their associates.

That did not surprise Slade; there were too many goings and comings in Marathon for any but the most outstanding characters to attract more than passing attention. Also, Veck Sosna was not the man to tie up with any local outfit. In that respect he was a lone wolf and gathered unto himself others of the same ilk.

When Slade repaired to the hotel, Leela greeted him with warmth, but resignedly.

"I suppose I'm getting used to it," she said. "Here today, gone tomorrow! Oh, well, I recall what my old grandmother, who always had a twinkle in her eye, used to say."

"What's that?" Slade asked smilingly.

"She used to say, 'Let the tomcat prowl; he'll come home over the back fence to mamma, after a while.' "

Slade shook with laughter. "Grandma was a philosopher, and wise in the ways of men," he commented. "I hope you inherited some of her astuteness."

"I think I did," Leela replied. "I hope so; I need it. Come on, let's go eat, and then we'll dance some if you're not too tired."

"Don't worry; you'll find out whether I'm too tired," he predicted, laughter in his eyes.

Meeting that laughing gaze, Leela blushed rosily.

The sheriff and the others had spread the story of the outwitting of the outlaws, and when he and Leela entered the saloon, Slade was the recipient of as many admiring glances as was his attractive companion. Sheriff Dobson was being urged to appoint him a deputy. The sheriff, who knew the truth, replied noncommittally that it might be a good notion.

Worthington and Elijah Crane joined them at their table and they ate together.

"Reckon we'd better be starting back home in the morning," the former remarked.

Slade nodded. He had no plans, hadn't the slightest notion where to look for Sosna. Might as well ride south as any direction. Besides, it would be necessary to return to Marathon within a few days to make sure the land deal had been consummated, and to pick up the papers. By which time he might have been able to formulate a plan of action against the outlaw.

"Then we'll dance some tonight," Leela said. "Again the stars," she whispered as, a little later, they circled the floor together. "It's about time!"

They rode the following morning, through the sun-washed glory of the autumn day, with the Big Bend at its best and showing what it could do weatherwise when it really took a notion. The mountain crests were like unheard thunder romping across the pastures of the sky, the valleys pools of violet edged with the gray-green of the mesquite and the sage. A streak of blazing white gleamed like a hazy silver ribbon, the crystal-encrusted shoreline of a desiccated salt lake. Higher and bolder loomed the broad cliffs, broken and fissured, the machicolated battlements of a stupendous castle of the days when giants walked the earth. Or so they seemed to Slade's imaginative eyes.

The sun climbed the long ladder of the heavens, paused for breath at the zenith and plunged down the opposite slant, drenching the western peaks with gold that flowed downward to meet the creeping shadows—the magic and the splendor of the wastelands, calling to those who knew their beauty and their terror, their loneliness and their peace. Slade breathed deeply, and turned to the girl at his side.

"Yes, I understand, too," she said softly, reading his thought. "But couldn't there be two wild ones instead of one?"

And El Halcón answered, "Maybe."

FIFTEEN

They found Espantosa Valley going strong when they completed the long ride. A remarkable amount of land had been cleared and some of the little houses were ready for occupancy, including Leela's.

"The boys thought they'd have it as a surprise for her," Mrs. Crane explained. "We moved in all the truck from the wagon; but honey, you can rearrange to suit yourself."

"I think it's perfect," said Leela, gazing about with shining eyes. "Don't you, Walt?"

"Couldn't be better," Slade declared. "I'd leave it just as it is. Yes, it's perfect." Mrs. Crane sniffed.

"No house is perfect unless there's a man in it," she said pointedly. "Well, that can be remedied."

Slade laughed; but Leela sighed. "Perhaps I can remove the roof and let the stars in," she said. Mrs. Crane looked puzzled, but apparently decided questions were out of order.

"Come on over to our place and eat," she said. "We haven't any roof yet, but the table and chairs are comfortable."

The farmers were enthralled by the account of their adventures in the course of the trip, and were relieved when Slade expressed the opinion that they no longer had need to fear attack by the outlaws, at least in the immediate future.

"The outfit is just about busted up, and it will take time to get another together," he concluded. Then he added, "And perhaps that can be prevented."

In fact, he did not believe that Sosna, even with a following at his back, would disturb the valley. He would have little or nothing to gain by doing so, and quite likely his thirst for revenge was tempered with respect for these Kentucky riflemen.

His greatest fear was that the outlaw, having suffered grievous defeat, would flee the section altogether. Then the chase would have to begin all over. Still, there were good pickings in the locale and plenty of recruits to be obtained by a leader of Sosna's proven ability. Maybe he would stick around, having perhaps decided that there was no use trying to run away from El Halcón, anyhow. Slade hoped so.

Slade spent the next several days in Espantosa Valley, assisting the farmers in their labors, despite their protests that he shouldn't be doing it. He gave them valuable pointers anent construction, draining and road building. Also, he showed them how to make the most of the water supply.

"Widening and deepening the streams to pools in various places may prove greatly to your advantage in case of a protracted dry spell such as you sometimes get in this country," he explained. "The Big Bend is all right, but you mustn't take liberties with it. All so-called wastelands are that way. Understand them and make them serve you. They'll do it if you have the know-how to take advantage of what they have to offer. Otherwise they can be deadly."

The nightly singfests were an institution with the farmers, and Slade led the singing. He showed little Tom Worthington how to tune his guitar and taught him new chords. And he spent more than a little time with Leela Austin.

"We'll keep you here and make a farmer of you

before we get through," motherly Mrs. Crane declared.

Altogether, he thoroughly enjoyed what was in the nature of a vacation. But all the time he was seeking an answer to the question which confronted him—where was Veck Sosna, and what deviltry was he planning?

That he was doing just that, Slade did not for a moment doubt. Sosna was not one to remain idle for any length of time. His boundless energy and his restlessness demanded action. Also, it was quite likely that he was in need of money, not having been very successful in accumulating a supply of late. Which in itself was enough to cause him to attempt some foray. He'd cut loose somewhere, in the near future.

El Halcón was right.

Old Sam Butterick was alone in his isolated ranchhouse. His hands had shoved a shipping herd to Marathon and would not be back until late in the evening, perhaps not until well after dark. Felipe, the cook, was out on the spread, checking, at the request of Len Ferguson, the range boss, some water holes that might need digging out. So there was nobody except Butterick around when the two strangers rode up to his veranda.

One was heavy-set, with an impassive face. The other, who had flashing black eyes, was very tall and broad-shouldered, and handsome in a dark feline way. His voice was modulated and musical, his smile charming.

"Will that trail over to the east we've been following from the north take us to Terlingua?" he asked.

"That's right," replied Butterick. "Keep on veering west all the time; don't turn east. Otherwise you'll hit the Comanche Crossing. Been riding for a spell?"

"For quite a spell," the tall stranger replied; "horses a mite fagged."

"Put 'em in the barn and give 'em a helpin' of oats, then come in for a snack," invited the hospitable rancher. "My boys are at Marathon, and the cook's out on the range, but I'll rustle you something."

The tall man murmured thanks. Both dismounted and led the horses to the barn. Exchanging significant glances, they returned to the ranchhouse, where Butterick was pottering around in the kitchen.

The tall man's eyes took in everything at a glance, then rested for a moment on a small iron safe standing in a corner of the living room.

In the kitchen, Butterick quickly threw together a cold meal with hot coffee to wash it down. He returned to the living room to fetch his guests. They rose from their chairs. The tall man took a long stride as Butterick turned; his arm rose and fell. A gun barrel thudded on the old man's skull and he fell to the floor to lie motionless, blood pouring from his split scalp.

The short man drew his gun and cocked it; but the other halted him with a gesture.

"We don't want any noise, and he's out for quite a while," he said. "Watch the door, now."

He knelt beside the safe, pressed his ear against the door and began twirling the combination knob.

"A school kid could open this old box without half trying," he remarked as he swung the door and began rifling the safe of its contents.

"Not very much, but it'll help until we tie onto some more," he said straightening up. "Get those sandwiches on the table and let's go."

Without a glance at the unconscious man whose hospitality they had so grossly violated, the unsavory pair left the ranchhouse, led their saddled and bridled horses from the barn and rode swiftly toward the Comanche Trail.

Felipe, returning to the ranchhouse shortly afterward, found his *patrón* bleeding and senseless on the floor. For a moment he stood in horror, then recovered his self-possession and knelt beside the stricken man.

The old Mexican had had plenty of experience with injuries in his time and he decided, after a brief examination, that the rancher was not badly hurt. Without delay he went to work on the wound. He had barely finished when

Butterick opened his eyes and swore feebly.

"Easy, *Patrón*," said the Mexican. "All is now well. Come, I will assist you to a chair; it is better that you sit. Thus the bleeding will cease more quickly. *Sí*, this is better. Now I will fetch you some coffee, which will also help."

When he returned with the coffee, he said, "And now tell me of how this evil was done."

Butterick told him, describing the two attackers. "They looked okay, but I reckon you can never tell," he concluded. "The last thing I remember is turning around and the roof fell on me."

"But why?" asked Felipe.

Butterick's eyes roved about the room, centered on the open safe.

"That's it," he said. "Busted open the box and cleaned it. Well, they only got a few hundred. Lucky the money the boys are bringing from Marathon wasn't in it; that would have been a real loss, the blankety-blanks!"

"*Patrón*," said Felipe, "El Halcón should know of this, and at once."

Butterick nodded his bandaged head. "I think you're right," he replied. "Chances are he's with his farmer *amigos* in Espantosa Valley."

"*Sí*, he will no doubt be there," agreed Felipe. "I will dare the terrors of that haunted place to bear the word to him."

"You don't have to worry about ghosts with El Halcón around," Butterick pointed out.

153

"*Sí*, that is so," Felipe said. "I will ride at once. I will take the sorrel *caballo*; he is swift and he is strong."

"Good notion," nodded Butterick. "Get me some more coffee and then hightail. I'm okay now, and the boys will be here before long."

The hands arrived shortly after dark and commented profanely when their boss told them what happened.

"Say!" exclaimed Ferguson, the range boss, "we met those two hellions, just this side of Marathon; they were headed for town. A tall one and a short one. Tall one had black eyes and black hair."

"That's right," replied Butterick.

"The mangy hyderphobia skunks!" growled Ferguson. "If we'd just known what happened!"

Felipe did ride fast, but it was past sundown when he reached the pass to Espantosa Valley. He instinctively crossed himself as he entered the gloomy gorge.

"But there is nothing to fear," he told the horse. "The Powers of Darkness flee before El Halcón."

He had no trouble locating Slade, for the evening singfest was in progress when he arrived. The Ranger listened quietly as he poured forth his story of the atrocity.

"*Gracias*, Felipe, for coming," he said when the Mexican paused. "You did the right thing."

"It was Sosna, all right," he told Van

Worthington. "Sosna and the other hellion who escaped us the other night. Well, I'm glad he's sticking around the section, anyhow. No sense in riding there tonight and rousing everybody up. And Felipe and his horse need rest. Little use in hurrying, for I haven't the slightest notion where to look for the devils. I'll make it first thing in the morning. Look after Felipe, Van, and day after tomorrow you and Lije had better ride to Marathon to pick up the land deal papers; I'll meet you there."

"Gone again, eh?" sighed Leela. "Well, as I said before, 'Gather ye rosebuds while ye may.' And the stars are shining."

Slade and Felipe left the valley shortly after daybreak and rode steadily until they reached the ranchhouse, where the news he received from the range boss was pleasing. For now at least he had a notion where Sosna was bound.

"I figure the sidewinder put one over on me," he told Butterick. "But I never dreamed he'd make a play for your place, although I should have taken into consideration that he's liable to do anything, especially the unexpected. And I should have described him more fully when I told you about him. Then you could have been on the watch for the hellion."

"I've a notion it's a good thing you didn't," replied the rancher. "If I'd showed suspicion or tried to resist when they rode up to the casa, the chances are I'd have gotten myself killed. As it is, things didn't work out so bad."

"Perhaps you're right," Slade conceded. "No doubt but you were lucky; perhaps because they didn't want to fire a shot that might have attracted attention. Sosna doesn't often leave a witness alive if he can help it."

Slade slept at the Butterick ranchhouse, departing early the next morning and riding steadily until he reached Marathon, where he proposed to spend the night.

"I'm just about convinced that pair is heading for Morton or somewhere thereabouts," he told Shadow. "Quite likely Sosna plans to pick up some recruits there to recoup his losses. Fairly probable that he has connections in that section. Well, we'll try and find out."

Arriving in Marathon, Slade stabled his horse, registered for a room at the hotel and repaired to the big saloon, the First Chance, for something to eat. He spent some time roving about the town and then returned to the saloon. As he expected, Van Worthington and Elijah Crane arrived soon after dark.

"Post office is closed for the day, so first thing in the morning we'll pick up the papers in the land deal; I'm pretty sure they are here by now."

"You riding back with us?" Worthington asked.

Slade shook his head. "I'm riding east for a spell," he replied; "but I'll be back."

"I'm scared you're not safe, riding around alone," Worthington demurred. "Those devils might be layin' for you."

"Nothing to worry about in this section, I'd say," Slade returned lightly. "That pair hightailed away from here."

Worthington was dubious. "Maybe so," he said, "but that feller Sosna 'pears to have a habit of doing just what you don't figure him to do."

Slade did not argue the point; it was unpleasantly true. However, he felt convinced that Sosna was heading for Morton or the neighborhood thereof as fast as he could get there. It was unreasonable to think that he'd tarry on the way.

"Don't worry about me," he told Worthington. "I'll be okay."

Worthington still appeared dubious, and so did old Lije, but they offered no further objection.

"Think you'll make it to Morton?" the former asked.

"Quite likely I will," Slade admitted.

"Well, if you do, tell my dance-floor gal I'll be coming for her mighty soon, now," Worthington requested. "Tell her the Reverend has his Book all ready to do a chore of hitching."

"I'll do that," Slade promised. "I've a notion she'll be glad to hear it."

"I hope so," said Worthington.

They spent some time in the saloon and then

157

decided to call it a day. Everything seemed peaceful enough, and they were tired.

"Want to be up early in the morning," said Worthington. "Maybe Lije and me can get started back home tomorrow."

Next morning the first business of the day was a visit to the post office. As Slade anticipated, the papers closing the land deal were there waiting for them. Worthington exclaimed with satisfaction as he scanned the documents.

"Now we're all set," he said. "Nothing to do but get busy and work hard; we'll make a go of it."

"I'm sure you will," Slade said. "Everything looks fine for you."

"And we owe it all to you," Worthington repeated. Elijah Crane nodded emphatic agreement.

"And I reckon we might as well be heading for the valley," he observed. "Take care of yourself, brother, and may the Good Lord prosper you in your undertaking."

SIXTEEN

After seeing the farmers off, Slade made preparations for his own longer ride. He packed his saddlebags with staple provisions and a helpin' of oats for Shadow and he made sure that he had plenty of spare ammunition.

"The way we've been burning it up hereabouts, we need a pack mule loaded with it," he told the horse.

Shadow's answering snort seemed to say, "You waste too darn much."

Slade chuckled, and did not argue.

These matters cared for, he headed east at a moderate pace, for he wished to save his mount against a possible emergency.

All day long he rode, lounging comfortably in his roomy Texas saddle with two cinches that did not cut the poor horse half in two, but alert and watchful nevertheless. For this was a wild land with little law other than what a man packed on his hip. At sundown he made camp on the bank of a little stream, where good grass grew. After cooking and eating his simple supper and cleaning up, he sat beside the dying fire, thinking.

He hoped he was right in his surmise that Veck Sosna was heading back to Morton. Of course he could be heading for most anywhere—east Texas, the Neches country, the Panhandle. If so, the arduous chase must start all over. However, he believed his hunch was a straight one, that Sosna would build up his band of outlaws in the Morton terrain with the intention of returning to the Big Bend country, where he would be safer from the forces of the law and where the pickings were good.

He wondered if Sosna would guess that

El Halcón was still on his trail. If such was the case, he would be doubly cautious. But there was a chance that he would not. Believing Slade himself wore the owlhoot brand, he would more likely conclude that he would remain with the farmers for a while. His remarks overheard by Slade while hiding in the attic of the hangout cabin seemed to justify such a conclusion. Well, time would tell. He rolled up in his blanket and went to sleep.

Awakening at dawn, he enjoyed a sluice in the cold waters of the stream. Feeling much refreshed, he cooked and ate his breakfast and gave Shadow a couple of handfuls of oats to top off his diet of grass. By a little after sunrise he had saddled up and continued on his way.

Gradually the nature of the country changed. The trail ran through chaparral that extended up the northern slopes, with occasional tall trees. On his right, however, began a strip of desert, sandy, stony and inhospitable, extending indefinitely to the south. Although the sun was still low in the sky, it was already shimmering with heat.

"A good section to keep away from," he told Shadow. "But so long as the trail runs through the brush the heat won't be too bad. So june along, horse, chances are there'll be better going before dark."

Perhaps his conclusion that Sosna was high-tailing to Morton made him a bit careless.

160

Otherwise, he told himself, what happened might have been averted.

He was passing beneath one of the tall trees that thrust massive branches and thick foliage across the trail. A slight rustling overhead caused him to look up quickly.

Not quickly enough! A rope swished down from above, a tight loop settled over his shoulders and was instantly jerked tight, hurling him from the saddle to strike the ground with stunning force. From behind the tree leaped a heavily built man, gun clubbed. As Slade strove to reach his Colts, the gun barrel crashed against his skull and he went limp.

From the tree dropped tall, flashing-eyed Veck Sosna.

"Got him!" he exulted. "It worked! I've waited a long time for this, the finish of El Halcón, and it isn't going to be a nice finish. Catch the horse."

Shadow had paused a few paces distant, looking back inquiringly. The stocky man reached for his bit iron, then yelled a curse and leaped back, blood streaming from his teeth-slashed hand. Shadow snorted, dashed into the brush and disappeared.

"Let the black devil go," called Sosna; "we don't need him. Come and give me a hand with this hellion. Out onto the desert with him, we won't need to go far. Already a bake oven out there. Grab his heels and let's go."

Together they carried the unconscious Ranger out onto the desert sands and stretched him on the ground. The stocky man hurried back into the growth and a few minutes later appeared leading two horses. Sosna immediately fumbled in the saddle pouch of one.

"Figured it would work and I have everything ready," he said. "Stretch his arms out—that's right."

Using a boulder for a hammer, he drove stout pegs deep into the ground, one beside each outstretched hand, and one beside each ankle. With short lengths of rope, he secured hands and ankles to the stakes, until Slade was spread-eagled on the sand. He dived into the saddle pouch again, drew forth a strip of rawhide about three inches wide, and a canteen. From the canteen he poured water on the rawhide, kneading and working it, adding more water and repeating the process, stretching the strip the while.

When the rawhide was thoroughly soaked, he deftly bound it around the Ranger's neck, making it snug and knotting it securely. He added a little more water, rocked back on his heels and surveyed his handiwork.

"That will do it," he said. "He should be coming out of it soon; we'll try and hasten the process."

He bathed Slade's temples with the water, chafed his wrists, sprinkled a few drops on his eyelids. Corking the canteen he set it aside. His gaze rested on the butts of Slade's guns protruding from the carefully worked and oiled cut-out holsters, and he gave an evil chuckle. Drawing the guns, he placed them beside the bound hands but a few inches out of reach of the Ranger's fingers, and chuckled again.

The stocky man spoke for the first time. "What the devil you doing that for?" he asked.

Veck Sosna let his burning gaze rest on the other's face for a moment. "Joyce," he said, "having but a modicum of intellect, and imagination not at all, you wouldn't be expected to understand. Perhaps, though, I can explain it so that even your walnut of a brain can grasp my purpose. The body is a thing finite, and as a thing finite so are its sensations, be they of pleasure or pain, finite also and must soon end. Whereas the mind is a thing infinite, and its sensations are also infinite—everlasting in its suffering, or seemingly so, no matter how long or short the actual time. Now our *amigo*, suffering bodily torture, will long for what would put a swift end to his sufferings—for that which lies almost within his grasp, almost but not quite, and his agonized mind will dwell with infinite longing on that which so near is yet so far and so add greatly to his suffering. Do you understand?"

"I don't understand what the devil you're

saying, but I sorta get what you mean," growled Joyce. "You mean he'll go plumb loco trying to reach those guns?"

"Wonderful!" exclaimed Sosna. "I almost feel that your case is not altogether hopeless, that there is reason lurking in you somewhere. That is precisely what I mean. Look! he's coming out of it."

Slade was. His eyelids fluttered, opened. He stared up blankly into the leering face of Veck Sosna. The outlaw's jeering voice roused him to full consciousness.

"So!" said Sosna. "So the great El Halcón fell for a moldy old trick. Really, I was quite surprised—agreeably surprised—when you rode under that tree without first carefully scrutinizing it. Well, even the smartest must stumble sometime."

Slade did not answer. Now that he had fully recovered his senses, his first real sensation aside from a splitting headache, was seething anger, directed at himself. It was a moldy old trick and his carelessness in falling for it was inexcusable. And he had no doubt that he would pay to the last pound of flesh for that moment of carelessness. Sosna was speaking again.

"So, seeing as you were sleeping so soundly, we brought you here and put you comfortably to bed in the warm sunshine. I even went to the length of placing that band of damp rawhide about your throat to protect it from sunburn. Of course as the rawhide dries it will constrict, tightening slowly until it may even make breathing somewhat difficult. It will be quite a while, however, before you grow weary of trying to breathe. You are strong; you should last until sunset.

"Well, we must be leaving you now. We have a little chore to attend to, but we'll be back in an hour or so to see how you are making out before we ride on. So don't be impatient and feel that you are being neglected. *Hasta luego*—till we meet again."

Sosna bent over, stared a moment at his helpless victim with eyes of awful gloating, then rose to his feet. He and his companion mounted their horses. A moment later Slade heard the clicking of their irons fading westward. He was left alone to face his predicament.

It was horrible enough. Slowly the rawhide would dry and tighten, a steel band crushing his larynx, closing his throat, until each gasping breath would be a torment indescribable. Turning his head he saw his guns where Sosna had placed them, just beyond his grasp. Unlike the stolid Joyce, he instantly understood the outlaw's devilish purpose, adding mental to physical torture. Instinctively, he was stretching his fingers toward the black butts. He jerked them back. The loose ends of the ropes which bound him curled over his fingers, but he could get no purchase

165

on them in the vain hope of loosening the knots.

Already he could feel the band about his throat fitting more snugly. Wouldn't take it long to tighten in the hot sun which was already adding to his discomfort. He closed his eyes against the intolerable glare, but they persisted in opening, searching about for the death that would come so slowly and horribly.

The minutes passed, the band tightened. Breathing became a little more difficult. And this was just the beginning. He wondered if his mind would snap before the agonizing end. Which would without doubt be a welcome relief. Not likely to, though; soon the pain would be too acute to allow a lapse into unconsciousness or delirium.

High in the brassy sky a black speck appeared, grew larger. Another joined it, and still another. Slade's straining eyes recognized them for what they were. Vultures! coming for the kill. They *knew!* No fooling those awful birds of ill omen. They knew the feast would soon be spread and were whetting anticipative beaks on the wall of the upper winds.

The rawhide band was tightening. Breathing was becoming more and more difficult. Now pain was stabbing his throat, steadily, growing sharper. He tugged and hauled at the ropes which bound his wrists; but the pegs were driven deep and did not budge. With his arms in their out-

166

stretched position, he could get no purchase, could not put forth his strength. Gasping with strain, sweat streaming down his face, he resisted the futile struggle, although he knew well it would begin again soon, not of his will but born of the frenzy of torture.

The vultures were still high in the blazing heavens, but they were wheeling lower, drifting down the long ladder of the sky rung by rung, their telescopic eyes fixed on the coming feast. They *knew!*

A sound broke the awful stillness of the wastelands, a high-pitched but musical sound—the plaintive whinny of a lonely and puzzled horse.

Shadow! Of course he had remained nearby. Now he was standing out on the sands, his great liquid eyes gazing wonderingly at the supine form of his master.

Slade managed a whistle through his parched and swollen lips. Shadow obediently trotted to him and thrust his muzzle into his hand. His fingers caressed the velvety nose. As he did so the loose end of the rope, some eight or ten inches in length, wripped up against the horse's nose. Shadow jerked his head back with a snort, then returned to the questing hand.

Suddenly a wave of hope swept over Slade. If he could just make the horse understand! He had taught Shadow to pull on a rope; it was a game they often played. Shadow would take the rope end in his teeth and Slade, a coil looped around his arm, would strive to draw the horse forward, and never could. Shadow would stand like a rock, then slowly step backward. And all El Halcón's great strength would be to no avail against the iron might of the black horse. Shadow would draw him forward easily, snorting in triumph. Now if he could only make the horse understand!

Again he wriggled the rope end, thrusting it toward the horse's nose as well he could with the small play allowed his fingers. Shadow looked suspicious, tentatively nosed the rope. Things didn't seem right to him—this was no way to play the game. Oh, well, there was no telling what this crazy Two-legs would want to do. It was the same old game that he liked, played from a different angle. A very absurd angle, Shadow seemed to think. He blew through his nose, then abruptly seized the rope with his teeth and began to pull, dragging hard on the peg, but at the same time dragging hard on Slade's arm. He felt as if it were being torn from the socket. Pain shot through his shoulder, then through the other shoulder as his right wrist was also drawn tight against the opposite peg. But the peg was moving!

"Take it, feller, take it!" he gasped, dragging back on the rope with his fingers.

Shadow seemed to understand, to begin to

enjoy the game played in this novel fashion; he put forth his strength. Slade gasped, for his shoulders were a flame of agony. The rawhide band about his throat was still tightening, pressing hard against his larynx, through which pain was also flowing. But he managed to gasp: "Take it! Take it!"

Shadow snorted, gave a hard pull. Slade almost fainted from the resulting stab of pain. Then he croaked unutterable relief, for the peg came out of the earth, flew up and rapped Shadow across the nose. The horse let go the rope and leaped back with a snort of anger. Slade writhed over sideways, got hold of the opposite peg with his freed hand. With all his remaining strength he tugged and hauled.

The peg resisted, for it was firmly fixed. Another hard tug and it loosened a little. Slade put forth his strength. The peg rasped out of the earth and both hands were free. Awkwardly he fumbled his clasp knife from a pocket, opened it with his teeth and slashed madly at the cords binding his ankles, quickly freeing them.

But he dared not try the knife on the rawhide band about his throat, not with his shaking hands. He tore at the knot which, tightening as the rawhide dried, stubbornly resisted his efforts. His nails were broken and bleeding when at last it loosened. He tore the band from about his throat and tossed it aside. Then, utterly overcome, he fell forward on his face.

And at that moment, thin with distance, sounded the hard, metallic clang of a rifle shot, again, and yet again.

SEVENTEEN

The threat of fresh peril jolted Slade out of the near-swoon into which he had fallen. He struggled to a sitting position, gulping great draughts of life-giving air. His strength was returning, his brain clearing. Making a supreme effort, he got to his feet to stand weaving. Drunkenly he reeled to where Shadow stood regarding him with wondering eyes.

"You did it, feller, you did it!" he gasped. With trembling hands he fumbled his canteen from the saddle pouch and took a few swallows of water. Then he poured a little in his cupped hands and gave it to Shadow. One more swallow—for he dared not drink too much—and he stoppered the canteen and restored it to the pouch.

"Come on, feller," he mumbled; "you've got to get in the clear."

Still walking unevenly, he led the horse into one of the thickets which flanked the trail. And as he did so, a plan was forming in his mind, a daring and dangerous plan, but one which he believed

170

might work. Sosna had said he would return in an hour or so, and the hour was almost up. And without a doubt the shooting he heard had to do with the "chore" the outlaw leader mentioned. Quite likely some unfortunate had died over to the west. With whatever hellishness he had in mind consummated, Sosna would undoubtedly return for a last look at his dying victim spread-eagled on the sands.

"Well, we'll be ready for him," he told Shadow. "Maybe this is the chance to get rid of the devil for good. Worth *taking* a chance to do."

Slade knew very well that in his present condition the sensible thing was to hightail away from there as fast as he could; but he felt that he and Sosna had to play the game out. He believed what he had in mind would work. A much better chance of it working than the alternative of holing up in the brush and waiting for the outlaws to ride into rifle range. Sosna was uncannily shrewd. Something might warn him. Also, it was unlikely that he would ride the trail into shooting distance. He was much more apt to head onto the desert a good way to the west, from where he could see his victim stretched out on the sand. And Slade knew he had to get Sosna close if he hoped to down him. His eyes were in bad shape from the sun glare and his strained shoulders and wrists would hamper his gun hand. He was in no condition to risk a long shot. Yes, he believed the stratagem would work. If it didn't, well, Sosna would rake in the chips; in this game it was winner take all. His mind made up, he returned to the desert and lay down in precisely the same position in which Sosna had left him, even to his guns resting on the sand just beyond hand reach, or so it would appear to anyone not too close.

Glancing up, he saw that the black dots that were the vultures had vanished.

"Better stick around, you feathered coyotes," he told them. "A good chance there'll be a table spread for you, after all."

The trail was hard and stony and Slade knew that in the great stillness of the wasteland the sound of horses' irons would carry a long ways. He strained his ears to catch the first rhythmic clicking that would herald the outlaws' approach. He was acutely uncomfortable, lying in the hot glare of the sun, which was mounting toward the zenith. His wrists and shoulders ached intolerably and his throat was frightfully sore. But he grimly endured the discomfort and waited.

Finally he heard it, the metallic beat steadily loudening. Abruptly it ceased. He waited, every nerve stretched to the breaking point, his eyes slanting westward.

From the growth perhaps four hundred yards distant bulged two horsemen who rode steadily in his direction. A flame of wrath enveloped him, blinded him for a moment. The sadistic devil was coming to gloat over his victim, to enjoy to the utmost his agonies. Well, he might well gloat from the other side of his face in a few more minutes.

The distance steadily shrank, the four hundred yards became three, two, one. Slade tensed for action. The hundred became sixty, dwindled to less than thirty. Then suddenly Sosna jerked his mount to a halt; his hawk eyes had discerned something that didn't seem just right.

Whirling over on his side, Slade seized his right-hand gun and fired again and again, steadying his hand by a terrific effort of the will.

The stocky man spun from his saddle as if struck by a mighty fist. Veck Sosna reeled, slumped forward, grabbing the horn for support. He whirled his mount and rode madly for the shelter of the brush. Slade emptied his gun after him, but his eyes were blurred, his hand shaking. He seized the second gun and pulled trigger even as Sosna vanished into the brush. Three more shots he sprayed into the chaparral, then held his fire, listening intently. The clashing of irons on the stones reached him, fading swiftly into the east. With a muttered oath he scrambled to his feet. His thought was to ride in pursuit; but he had reached the limit of his endurance. The strength born of excitement was draining away as the reaction set in; he could barely stand. He drew a deep breath of the hot air, which rasped his sore throat, cast a glance at the motionless form of the dead man on the sands, summoned the last of his powers for a final effort and shambled to where Shadow was concealed.

After what seemed an eternity of suffering he reached the horse and leaned against its shoulder, utterly spent. Shadow craned his neck and whickered softly.

"Thanks, more than I can tell you, feller," Slade muttered. "You saved me. But that devil got away, as usual. I think I nicked him pretty hard, though, from the way he slumped, but folks say he already has enough lead in his body to make a pig, so I'm afraid another ounce won't discommode him too much."

Fumbling the canteen from the pouch, he uncorked it and drank deeply, giving what was left to Shadow. Then he sat down with his back to a tree, rolled a cigarette and smoked it slowly to a short butt, while Shadow cropped the scanty grass, which he seemed to think better than nothing.

Feeling much better, although still far from his normal self, Slade pinched out the butt, replaced the bit, tightened the cinches and mounted. Gaining the trail, he turned Shadow's nose west. The shooting he had heard over there prior to the reappearance of the outlaws needed a mite of investigation. He was anxious to learn what it was about and dreaded what he would find.

His fears were justified before he had covered a mile. In the distance stood a buckboard, the two horses browsing on the leaves which bordered the trail. As he drew near, he saw that a man was lying motionless on the ground, another huddled down against the dashboard of the vehicle. No doubt but both were dead.

Beside the buckboard, Slade dismounted, still unsteady on his feet, and gave the pair a once-over. The man against the dashboard, no doubt the driver, wore overalls and a soft shirt open at the throat. The other was dressed in what the rangeland called "store clothes," even to a starched collar and a black string tie. Quite likely a clerical worker, Slade concluded.

For a moment he pondered the situation. The dead men had been headed east when the outlaws dry-gulched them. Therefore somewhere along the line he should be able to obtain information relative to them. He managed to move the driver from where he was wedged against the dashboard and onto the seat. Then he approached the other, marveling at the effort required to lift the slight form. After a struggle he got him also onto the seat. He roped the limp forms securely in place, so that they sat hunched over with chins resting on their breasts, as if in sleep. Then he mounted Shadow, with difficulty, and rode east, leading the buckboard horses, the two stark forms on the seat nodding and lurching grotesquely.

Opposite where the body of the outlaw lay on the sands he pulled up and dismounted. Near the dead man his horse nosed about in search of provender. It bore a brand Slade did not recognize. Summoning all of his remaining strength, he managed to drag the carcass through the brush and wedge it at the feet of the pair on the seat. He caught the horse and tied it to the rear of the vehicle. Mounting was again a chore, but he finally made it, wedging his feet firmly in the stirrups. The grim procession moved on.

As he rode, Slade realized that he was hurt more than he had thought. There was a haze before his eyes, his movements were jerky, lacking in their usual smooth co-ordination. His shoulders ached unceasingly and breathing was difficult. Dully he wondered if Sosna was lying in wait for him somewhere, although he thought that unlikely. *He* might be hurt more than a little, too. Slade was of the opinion he would continue to where he could obtain medical attention or could care for his wound himself, as he was perfectly capable of doing were it not too serious. Anyhow, he'd have to take his chance with a possible dry-gulching. And he was too worn and weary to care much what happened.

Hour after hour he rode, the reins of the buck-board horses twined about his arm, sometimes lifting his heavy eyes to scan the trail, giving Shadow his head. He knew that he was very close to the dank borderland of delirium induced by pain and physical exhaustion; but he grimly held on.

It was nearly sunset when he sighted a huddle of buildings ahead and to the left of the trail. Smoke boiled from a tall stack and there came to his ears the hum of machinery. Evidently it was one of the small mines of low-grade ore that dotted the hills in the section. In front of the buildings he pulled to a halt.

A man beside one of the buildings stood staring in astonishment at the grisly caravan. Slade dismounted and beckoned him to approach. He gestured to the bodies on the seat as the man drew near.

"See if you know them," he said.

The other, muttering, bent down and peered into the dead faces, and straightened up with a jerk.

"My God!" he exclaimed. "It's Herb Parr and Mr. Gavin!" He whirled about and ran to one of the buildings, shouting loudly,

"Mr. Benton! Mr. Benton!"

An elderly man, neatly dressed, appeared questioningly in the doorway. The other gabbled to him almost incoherently. Benton hurried down the steps and to where Slade stood hanging onto the saddle horn for support.

"Are—are they dead?" he gasped.

"If they're not, they're doing a wonderful job

of playing 'possum," Slade replied dryly. "Yes, they're dead. You know them?"

"They're Gavin, my paymaster, and one of our drivers," the other said. "I'm Jim Benton, the manager here. Can you tell me what happened?"

Slade told him, in detail, starting with his own capture on the trail. A look of horror spread over the mine manager's face as he listened.

"And they intended to leave you there to die in that awful fashion," he muttered. He glanced keenly at Slade.

"You don't look good, cowboy," he said. "Your throat's like a piece of raw beefsteak. Come with me and I'll get you coffee and food. We'll take care of your horse and the others." He called a name and a man who had joined a growing group nearby came forward.

"It's okay, Shadow, go with him," Slade told the black. The man led him to a nearby barn, while others began unhitching the buckboard horses. Still others lifted the bodies from the seat.

"Take them into the office, all three of them," said Benton. "Now you come along with me, cowboy; we can talk while you eat."

Gratefully, Slade accepted the invitation, following the manager into what was a cook shanty. Benton sat silent while an old cook plied the Ranger with food and steaming coffee. Slade ate and drank, feeling his strength return. His mind cleared and he began feeling something like himself again.

Finally, with a sigh of satisfaction, he pushed back his plate and began manufacturing a cigarette.

"Feeling better, eh?" commented Benton. "Now just take it easy for a spell. You've been through a harrowing experience, and there's a limit to what even a big, powerful man like yourself can take."

"So I learned," Slade conceded, with a wan grin. Benton chuckled.

"I learned that long ago," he said. "Now, Mike, the cook, will give you a once-over. He's a bit of a doctor and always has a lot of stuff around. He'll have something that will be good for your throat, and liniment for your shoulders. Take over, Mike."

The old cook shuffled forward, bearing bottles and jars.

"Shirt off," he directed. Slade obeyed.

"Hold still," said Mike, evidently a person of few words. But his gnarled old fingers were deft and gentle as a woman's as he treated Slade's bruised and lacerated throat with a soothing ointment and patted liniment on his shoulders. With a critical glance at his handiwork, he stepped back and began gathering up his medicaments.

"Thank you, Mike," Slade said.

"Good practice, need it," grunted Mike and

shambled away. Slade turned to the manager, after donning his shirt.

"And now, Mr. Benton, I'd like to ask you a few questions. Do you know why your men were killed—was it robbery?"

"Yes, it was robbery," Benton answered. "They were bringing payroll money from Marathon— two thousand dollars and better. We do our banking at Marathon, although Morton, to the east, is closer. We have another and larger mine near Marathon."

"I see," Slade nodded. "And Sosna caught on and was laying for them, just as he laid for me. Good timing on his part, but he does things that way."

"Just who is this man Sosna?" the manager asked.

"He's a devil," Slade replied grimly. "A Panhandle outlaw who's cut a swath across half of Texas. I've been trailing him for a couple of years, but I never seem able to really catch up with him, although once I thought I had."

Benton shot him a shrewd glance. "I think I understand," he said slowly. "Well, here's hoping your bullet found a vital mark."

"I fear it didn't," Slade answered. "He's a hard one to kill and he always seems to get the breaks."

"He'll finally get one that will break his blasted neck," Benton prophesied. "I suppose I should notify Sheriff Stockley at Morton of what happened, and without delay?"

"Yes," Slade replied. "I'd ride on to Morton myself, only I hardly feel up to it right now."

"You'll do nothing of the sort," Benton declared flatly. "You're going to take it easy, and whenever you say the word, there's a comfortable bed waiting for you. I'll send a man for Stockley. Excuse me a minute, and when I come back we'll have some coffee together, right?"

He hurried out and Slade heard him calling orders to somebody.

"Fellow will be on his way in half an hour," he announced when he returned, a few minutes later. "He'll have Stockley here by noon tomorrow, or a little after. Rustle the coffee, Mike."

A little later, Slade stretched out on a comfortable bed in the manager's quarters and slept soundly despite his various aches and pains. Morning found him still stiff and sore but much improved. After a hearty breakfast which Mike prepared and garnished with pithy remarks that caused Slade to chuckle, he contacted Benton and they inspected the mine workings together.

EIGHTEEN

Slade surprised the manager with a few suggestions that appealed to Benton and which he announced his intention of adopting.

"You seem to know a good deal about mining, Mr. Slade, for a—a cowhand," he commented.

"I've had a little experience around mines," Slade replied.

"So I gather," Benton said dryly.

Sheriff Stockley showed up shortly after noon. "I might have known it," he sighed resignedly as he shook hands with Slade. "Figured it was you from the fellow's description. Knew darn well it must be when he told me there was a passel of carcasses awaiting inspection. Benton, you'll be lucky if the mine don't blow up or something before he leaves. Trouble just follows him around. I thought he'd gone for good, but here he shows up again like a bad *peso.* Well, they say there's no peace for the wicked, and I reckon I've got a lot to account for. How did you make out with your farmers, Walt? Did you get 'em to that valley with the loco name you told them about? You can tell me about it while we eat."

Slade regaled his listeners with an account of the trip to Espantosa Valley and the subsequent happenings. The sheriff swore his amazement.

"So it really was those hellions dressed up to look like Apaches, just as you said, eh? Well, it seems you're never wrong. And you and the uppity old preacher made out okay together, eh?"

"A man to ride the river with," Slade replied. The sheriff chuckled.

"And how about the pretty girl you had a row with first off?" he asked.

"She's okay to ride the river, too," Slade smiled. Stockley chuckled again.

"And is young Worthington really coming back for Katy, that little dance-floor girl?"

"He sure is," Slade replied.

"She'll be glad to hear it," said the sheriff. "She don't talk about anything else. She's okay and will make him a good wife. As I told you once before, old Carson won't have any other sort in his place. And I suppose you'll still be riding Sosna's trail."

"I will," Slade replied grimly.

"You'll get him, sooner or later, no doubt about that," declared Stockley.

"I haven't had much luck so far," Slade replied morosely. "Yesterday he darn near got me. If he'd been satisfied with just a plain killing instead of one by torture, he would have."

"But he didn't," the sheriff returned cheerfully. "Guess it just wasn't intended."

"About the only explanation I can think of," Slade conceded. "Destiny, using my horse as an instrument; Shadow deserves his share of credit. But if I'd managed to down Sosna yesterday, I'd have recovered Mr. Benton's payroll money; he was packing it, of course."

"Don't let that worry you," Benton said cheerfully. "It was insured. Let the insurance company send one of their smart operators to run it down."

"And be short an operator, that is if he happens to run into Sosna," grunted the sheriff. "Well, I'd like to take a look at the hellion Walt brought in."

"Might go through his pockets while you're at it," Slade suggested. "I left them for you to examine. Chances are you'll find nothing of any consequence, however; that sort seldom carries anything that would tie him up with somebody or something. Look at the brand on the horse, too; I don't recognize it."

They repaired to the office where the bodies were laid out. An examination of the outlaw's pockets produced nothing of significance aside from some money, though not a great deal.

The sheriff gazed sadly at the other two dead faces. "Did they leave any relations?" he asked. Benton shook his head.

"None that I know of," he replied. "Gavin showed up here a few years back, looking for work. I learned he was an educated man and put him in the office; he handled all the book work. Was efficient and dependable, but I never heard him mention any relatives. The same goes for Parr, who was a good driver and handled one of the ore wagons."

The sheriff nodded his understanding. "Gone to Texas" was a phrase that applied to men who, for one reason or another, desired to lose their past identity.

"Well, I'll pack them to Morton and hold an inquest," he said. "Guess that's all I can do for them."

"You can have the light wagon," said Benton. "I'll send a driver along to bring it back."

"Much obliged," the sheriff accepted the offer. "You riding with me, Walt?"

"Might as well," the Ranger said. "May be able to learn something there. Sosna was headed in that direction, so far as I know."

"Sure you feel up to it, Mr. Slade?" Benton asked. "Your throat still doesn't look too good to me."

"It'll be okay, thanks to Mike," Slade answered. "It feels a lot better than it did before he worked on it; he knows his business. An excellent cook, too."

"Gets plenty of experience in both lines," said Benton. "Our rock busters sure eat, and they're always having something happen to them, especially when they go to town for a payday celebration. Skinned heads and swollen noses are commonplace with them."

"Don't I know it," grumbled the sheriff. "They're always getting into a shindig, usually of their own starting. Hard to tell which is worse, rock busters or cowhands. Well, I suppose we might as well get started. Be midnight before we make it to town."

The bodies were placed in the light wagon. Slade and the sheriff saddled their horses and rode in front.

"I'll attend to the burying of my men," Benton told them as they got under way. "You can have the other one for a keepsake, Stockley."

"Might be worse," responded the cheerful sheriff. "I once knowed a feller who cut off ears and smoked 'em. Used to carry 'em in his vest pockets. Would some time drop one in a glass of whiskey at the bar. Said it pickled 'em and kept 'em fresh-looking. Funny, but somehow that feller wasn't overly popular. Let's go!"

During the ride, Slade was silent and pre-occupied most of the time. His physical ailments were on the mend, but mentally he was depressed and beset by a sense of frustration. Things weren't going right at all. He wondered moodily if he was right in his guess that Sosna would head for Morton, there to pick up a possible remnant of his followers and go on the rampage again. Slade believed he would. He also believed that very likely he would circle back to the Big Bend country. And where the devil to look for him in that vast wasteland!

Then again, he might keep on going after a pause at Morton and lose himself somewhere in the even vaster terrain of Texas. "Gone to Texas!" Plenty of men with pasts that would not bear scrutiny found sanctuary in sparsely settled sections where no questions were asked, and quite often their pasts never caught up with them. Well, Veck Sosna had a past, all right, but he was always very busy making the present into a reprehensible past.

Slade felt that his thought processes were getting decidedly scrambled, which didn't make him feel any better. Then his sense of humor came to the rescue and he chuckled to himself. Pitting one's wits against Sosna's was an excellent way to get "scrambled" in more ways than one. However, after carefully analyzing past performances, he felt that he was one up on Sosna. At least he had him on the run, which was something. Now it was up to him to keep him on the run, and eventually catch up with him for the final showdown. By the time the lights of Morton were twinkling in the distance he was again his normally cheerful self.

Sheriff Stockley, who had learned to understand and respect the Ranger's moods, also perked up.

"After we dispose of our cargo, suppose we

drop over to Carson's place for a snort or two," he suggested. "Things usually lively there."

"A good notion," Slade agreed. "I want to deliver Worthington's message to Katy, and I figure I can use a snort myself, now that I can swallow in comparative comfort once more. Guess, though, I should be thankful that I'm able to swallow at all. Sure looked for a while like I never would again, at least in this world."

"That hyderphobia skunk!" growled the sheriff. "I'd sure like to line sights with him. I can sorta put up with a clean killer even though I don't approve of him, but that sort! Killin's too good for him."

"Just the same, his lust for cruelty is a weakness that may be his undoing," Slade commented.

"You're right," the sheriff nodded. "Because of it, he's still got El Halcón on his trail."

After reaching Morton, they roused up the local undertaker and left the bodies in his care. After that they repaired to the saloon.

Old man Carson, who successfully hid a lot of heart beneath a crusty exterior, greeted them warmly and at once called Katy to join them at a table.

The dance-floor girl was a gay little thing with laughing eyes and a nice mouth. The laughter changed to a soft glow as Slade relayed Worthington's message.

"I can hardly wait," she said. "I like it here,

188

and Mr. Carson is wonderful to all the girls, but there's not much of a future for a girl in this line. Being a farmer's wife will be a whole lot nicer. And that poor little boy of Van's needs somebody to mother him."

"He and Van are both getting a break," Slade declared. The sheriff nodded emphatic agreement.

The place was lively all right and there was plenty of business. Katy declined the offer of a drink and returned to the floor. Slade and the sheriff were discussing their second when the Ranger suddenly had an idea.

"Wonder if we could locate the doctor at this time of night?" he asked.

"Sure, he stays up to all hours; his business is usually good at night," replied Stockley. "Why? You not feeling right?"

"Feeling fine now," Slade answered. "I'm of the opinion that Sosna may have needed medical attention; I've a notion I nicked him pretty hard, from the way he slumped in the hull. Perhaps the doctor can tell us something."

"By gosh, you're right!" exclaimed Stockley, and downed his drink. "Let's go. We can come back later."

They found the doctor, a white-whiskered old fellow with shrewd eyes, in his office. Slade was introduced and proceeded to describe Veck Sosna. The doctor nodded his grizzled head.

"Yep, reckon it was him, big tall feller with mighty bright black eyes. Well spoken. Came in late last night. Had a hole through the left arm flexor muscle, the biceps. Said a steer he was bulldogging rammed a horn through it. Maybe so, but in my opinion that *steer* had a lead-tipped horn. Nope, don't know where he went. I didn't ask him any questions—not my business to do so. I patched him up—he wasn't hurt overly bad—and he left. Had his horse hitched at the rack outside, under the street light, a big chestnut. Forked it and rode off down the street. You looking for him, John?"

"Yep," replied the sheriff. "You're lucky to be alive. Wonder he didn't kill you just for the fun of it; he's that sort."

"Gun slingers don't often plug a sawbones—got too much use for them," the doctor replied calmly. "He was a salty-looking jigger, though, all right. Good hunting! Glad to know you, Mr. Slade. Drop in whenever you're of a mind to, even if you don't need to have lead mined out of you."

"I've a notion he is plenty salty if necessary," Slade chuckled, talking of the doctor, as they walked back to Carson's place. "Sosna might have gotten his throat slit with a scalpel if he'd made a move toward him."

"Pity he didn't," growled the sheriff. "Well, you were right when you figured the hellion would head for Morton."

"Yes, that's something," Slade conceded. "But the big question is, where did he go?"

"May be hanging around," said Stockley. "Anyhow, you'd better keep your eyes skinned and make sure he doesn't see you before you see him. I feel the need of another drink."

The bar was lined two deep, but Carson found them a small table in a corner near the dance floor. The sheriff ordered a drink. Slade settled for coffee. Ensconced in comfort, they sat watching the colorful scene and conversing on various subjects.

Eventually, however, the talk drifted back to Veck Sosna and his nefarious activities.

"From what you tell of him, I figure he'll bust loose with something before long," Stockley remarked thoughtfully. "Now if we can just figure out what would tempt him to make a try for it."

"Yes, then we might anticipate his move and counteract it," Slade said. "I can't see a wide-looping of some cows; I'm pretty well convinced that he hasn't enough men left to successfully pull one worth his while. There are no stages packing money that run in this section, and I hardly think he'd try another train robbery."

"Not many of them ever pack money in this section, except for a delivery to the bank just before paydays, and then they're always mighty well guarded," observed the sheriff.

"Whatever it is, it will be something

unexpected, daring and out of the ordinary, or so I read the cards," Slade said. "For all his shrewdness, I've observed that he works in a methodical way, which helps one to anticipate his moves; except when all of a sudden he branches out into something new, which does happen occasionally. Take that robbery of John Butterick over by the Comanche Trail. I never knew him to tackle a ranchhouse in such a manner, with no previous planning and only guessing that there might be a haul; ranchers as a rule don't have much money lying around loose.

"Of course, though," he added, "right then Sosna was desperate for some ready money, having failed to hold on to what he acquired from the train robbery. Next time, though, I figure it will be something really big, something that will perhaps enable him to flee the country, which I have a feeling he may be planning to do. In the interior of Mexico he would be safe."

"You may have something there," conceded Stockley. "I've a notion you've got him on the run."

"Perhaps," Slade agreed. "The chore is, however, to keep him that way, and he's a slippery customer."

A period of silence followed, the sheriff watching the activities at the bar, Slade pondering the problem that confronted him. Suddenly he asked,

"John, when is payday for the spreads and the mines? Pretty close, isn't it?"

"Why, yes," Stockley replied. "Just three days off, to be exact. Why?"

"Oh, just wondering," Slade replied evasively. In his mind an idea had birthed, but he did not care to take the sheriff into his confidence, at least not yet. Stockley would want to be in on anything he might undertake, and he wasn't sure that he wanted company on the chore he'd be setting for himself if the various ramifications involved would make the idea plausible.

"Well," he said, a few moments later, "if *Señor* Sosna figures to pull something tonight, he'll have to do it by himself. I'm going to bed. Feel a mite worn."

"No wonder," nodded the sheriff. "An average person would be laid up for a week if they'd gone through what you did. Feel a bit tuckered myself, just thinking about it. Let's go—plenty of room at my place. It is getting late—soon be morning. Let's go."

NINETEEN

Thoroughly worn out, Slade slept soundly till midmorning. He repaired to Carson's place for some breakfast, and after eating, strolled about the town, pausing across the street from the

Morton bank, which was somewhat isolated and close to what was locally called the north-south Fort Stockton Trail.

For several minutes he studied the building. Then he walked slowly to the corner and turned south, paralleling the structure.

The rear of the bank building fronted on a narrow and unlighted alley. Slade turned into the alley and walked even more slowly. He saw that there was a back door and a window opening onto the alley. The window was barred with iron, the door closed and probably locked.

Running into the alley, like the leg of a T, was a second and even narrower alley also devoid of street lights. Its mouth was almost opposite the bank building. Both alleys were lined with warehouses, now bustling and busy. At night, however, they would be dark and deserted.

Slade studied the layout thoroughly, then turned about and walked to the trail, which wound through the outskirts of the town and only a block from the bank, running due south to the distant Rio Grande, a very convenient getaway route for anybody fleeing the country. It passed through a wild and practically uninhabited country, then skirted the rugged Bullis Gap Range and, farther south, the sinister Dead Horse Mountains, to reach the river just east of grim Boquillas Canyon.

Yes, a true wasteland down there, made to order

for hunted men, with the sanctuary of the country of *mañana* beyond.

Heavy with thought, Slade walked back to the central part of the town. He tried, as before, to put himself in the place of Sosna, to try to gauge the outlaw's reactions as his own. His course, the Ranger believed, was fairly obvious. One more good haul and then flight to safety.

Good reasoning. Only, Veck Sosna did not always reconcile with good reasoning. However, this time Slade believed his hunch was a straight one. Anyhow, he would play it and hope for the best.

Morton was quiet, comparatively speaking, that night, catching its collective breath for the turbulence of day after tomorrow and payday. Late that afternoon a number of canvas sacks had been unloaded from the westbound local train and had, under guard, been transported to the bank. Tomorrow the representatives of the mines and the ranches would be in town to draw money with which to pay off their workers. Then next day the big bust—maybe. Slade chuckled at the thought that the celebration might well depend on his activities during the next twelve hours or so.

What he termed a hunch, was really the result of painstaking deduction based on his knowledge of Sosna's methods and ways of thought and action. He had undoubtedly come to Morton on a definite mission. To recruit more followers for his decimated outfit? At first Slade was inclined to think so, but more mature reflection discarded the assumption. He did not believe that Sosna had left more than one or two of his men in Morton when he headed west, who would relay the word of approaching wagon trains or anything that promised loot. Sosna was thoroughly conversant with all the activities of the cow and mining town. He would know when payday was due and that the money would be in the bank two days previous. And it would make an excellent haul. The old vault in which it was kept would offer little difficulty to the experienced safe-cracker, something very uncommon to the rangeland, and against which no special provisions were ever taken.

All theory, of course, but Slade believed it to be sound theory that would translate into fact. Anyhow, he was going to play his hunch to the hilt. And he had a premonition that this would be showdown, the end, one way or another, of the feud between Veck Sosna and El Halcón, already becoming one of the sagas of the West.

The hours passed and before midnight the streets, even the busier ones, were practically deserted. In the saloons the bartenders yawned and glanced at the clock. The dance floors had already closed down.

Morton was seeking rest, girding against the

196

onslaught of day after tomorrow and its golden flood.

Shortly before midnight, Slade got the rig on Shadow and rode west. On a rise a mile distant he pulled up and for long minutes studied the back trail. Confident that he was not wearing a tail, he circled the town and entered the south mouth of the narrow alley which bisected the one running past the rear of the bank. He dismounted and led the horse, its slow hoofbeats making scarcely any sound on the thick dust. A dozen yards back of the alley's north mouth he left Shadow, the split reins trailing, knowing that the horse would make no noise and would be ready to hand in case of need. This time there would be no slip-up were a chase in order. He silently made his way to the alley mouth and took up his post in the gloom at the base of a blank warehouse wall. From where he stood he could make out the outlines of the window and the back door. Nobody could approach that door without being observed, a door that would offer scant resistance to Sosna's exhaustive knowledge of locks and how they were to be outwitted.

The minutes dragged past, totaled a full hour, and Slade began to grow acutely uneasy. If anything was going to happen, it should have already happened. Looked like his hunch wasn't a straight one, after all. But all the while a presentiment of evil was building up in his mind.

The unexplainable sixth sense that develops in men who ride much alone with danger as a stirrup companion was stirring, was voicing its soundless warning. He glanced over his shoulder, although he knew well that did somebody come up the alley behind him, Shadow would inevitably voice a warning by blowing softly through his nose. With the black horse where it was, nobody could take him by surprise from the rear. He again fixed his attention on the closed door.

And Sosna at that very moment, with his uncanny genius for doing the unexpected, was putting it over on him.

But for once the outlaw leader was just a mite too cautious. His habit of always providing himself with a bolt hole, if at all possible, was the one small flaw in his daring and carefully worked out plan. That, added to Slade's concentration on the back door of the bank. His keen eyes saw the door move a little, although nobody was anywhere in sight. It moved, opening inward a tiny crack, which remained a paler streak in the gloom.

El Halcón stared unbelievingly. The only possible explanation of the phenomenon was that somebody was *inside* the building and had opened the door from the inside!

Yes, that was it. Sosna, ignoring the obviously

greater safety of the dark alley, had walked boldly to the front door, unlocked it with a key made for that purpose, and entered as if he owned the place.

For a moment Slade was paralyzed to inaction by the very audacity of the rapscallion, at which he even then found time to marvel. And now he noticed that the panes of the barred window appeared just a little paler, as if there was a faint gleam of light filtering through them. He snapped out of it and glided across the alley to the door, hands close to the butts of his guns. Reaching the door, he paused, peering and listening.

To his ears came a sound, scarcely louder than the purr of a contented kitten, but with a faint metallic rasp to it that never originated in a cat's throat. The whine of a drill eating into metal.

Slade hesitated. Should he slip around and enter by way of the front door? He knew that the position of the vault was such that anybody working on it would have his back to the front door, whereas he would have a side view of the rear door. But the wily Sosna might well have locked the front door against possible interruption from that quarter, unlocking and standing the back door ajar as an escape precaution.

Viewed with Sosna's unusual attributes taken into consideration, the whole set-up was a logical development. Usually the only way a safe was opened in cattle country was with dynamite or a sledge-hammer and chisel. Both methods entailed too much noise to be practical under present conditions. But to a safe-cracker of Sosna's proven ability, drilling out the combination knob and opening the vault was a commonplace chore, circumstances being what they were. Nobody had ever robbed the Morton bank, so of course nobody ever would. Such a contingency was not given any thought. Sosna could expect to have plenty of uninterrupted time to do the chore. And right now he was busily accomplishing the feat.

All this raced through Slade's mind during the fleeting instant he stood beside the opened door. Sosna's plan was well nigh perfect except for one imponderable; that elusive imponderable which would very likely prove his undoing was El Halcón.

Loosening his guns in their sheaths, Slade stepped back; no use trying to make a quiet entrance, not with Veck Sosna's almost supernatural senses alert for any interruption. He hurled himself forward, striking the door with his shoulder. It flew open with a bang and he was inside the bank.

There were two men facing the vault door, on which Veck Sosna was busy with a hand drill; already three overlapping holes punctured the steel next to the knob, on which the slender beam of a dark lantern was focused. Beside him loomed the second man, shorter, of more massive build

Both whirled at the crash of the opening door. Slade's voice rang out: "Elevate! In the name of the State of Texas—" The room fairly exploded to a whirlwind of action. Sosna leaped back like a great cat, snapping shut the slide of the lantern with a perfectly coordinated sweep of movement; darkness swooped down like a thrown blanket, through which gushed lances of orange flame. Slade went sideways along the wall, dropped to his knees, shooting with both hands. Lead yelled over his head, thudding into the wall.

A gasping, gurgling cry knifed through the uproar, a thud and a wild thrashing about. The front door crashed open. Footsteps pattered on the sidewalk. Slade leaped to his feet and bounded forward. He tripped over a body and pitched headlong, striking the floor with a force that knocked all the breath from his lungs and almost paralyzed his limbs. As he struggled to rise, he heard a click of fast hoofs fading eastward. Surging erect, he reeled for a moment, caught his balance and leaped over the body, racing for the back door. As he sped across the alley, he heard shouts in the distance, drawing nearer. Sheriff Stockley would arrive shortly and would take in the situation at a glance. Slade knew very well who was forking that horse which had vanished around the corner; the Sosna luck was still holding.

Hurling himself into the saddle, he sent Shadow

charging to the Fort Stockton Trail. Far ahead to the south, his big chestnut going like the wind, was Veck Sosna. Slade settled himself in the saddle; his voice rang out: "Trail, Shadow, trail!"

The great black bounded forward; the last grim race was on.

The chestnut was a splendid animal—Veck Sosna was without a peer as a judge of horse flesh—but Slade had every confidence in the speed and endurance of his own mount.

"We'll get him, feller," he muttered. "That is if he doesn't pull another miracle of some sort out of the hat."

The late moon climbed higher, pouring its ghostly light over the wild rangeland and the hills and mountains to the west. Thickets stood out like fuzzy-edged ebony carvings. The trail was a ribbon of pale silver unwinding from the spool of eternity. The miles whispered back under Shadow's flying hoofs. He was holding his position. In fact, he was doing a little better, gaining a few yards in each hundred.

Sosna vanished around a brush-lined curve. Slade's hand remained loose on the bridle. He did not believe Sosna would pause to attempt a dry-gulching. He was heading for the Rio Grande and Mexico, and nothing would stop him except a well-placed bullet. Slade estimated the distance to the beginning of the curve, urged Shadow to greater speed.

They careened around the bend, Slade alert and watchful, a hand close to his gun butt. The trail straightened out and there was Sosna, still well ahead, but not so much so as before. Slade saw the white blur of his face as he turned in the saddle to gaze back at his pursuer. He was using his quirt on the chestnut now, but Shadow was still closing the distance. Slade reached down and made sure his Winchester was free in the boot. Before long he should be able to risk a shot.

Not yet, however, to do so would mean to sacrifice precious distance gained. One well-directed slug would do the work, but that one must be the first. Almost at hand was the culmination of the years of effort. Yes, the long tally of the years was complete. He spoke to the flying black. Shadow snorted, slugged his head above the bit and his thunder irons beat out a faster tempo.

Another curve, and another gamble that Sosna would not draw rein. He didn't. Again the straightaway, and the big chestnut was losing ground. He had given his all, and it wasn't quite enough.

Now there were hills to the left, rugged, craggy hills, and a half mile or so ahead they were split by a canyon mouth which yawned darkly between beetling cliffs. And now Shadow was gaining steadily.

Again Sosna turned in the saddle for a long

look at his nemesis. Directly ahead was the canyon mouth. He swerved the chestnut and vanished into the opening. Slade uttered an exasperated oath. If the gorge was heavily brush-grown, a hazardous game of hide and seek was in the making. He reached the canyon, careened into it and gave a sigh of relief. Only a scattering of low bush dotted the gorge floor, which had a slightly upward slant. And he saw now that he was following a trail, a very old trail that showed no signs of recent usage. But Sosna must surely know where he was going, and seeing that direct flight was hopeless, was seeking some sanctuary. Slade urged his mount with voice and hand, and drew the rifle from its scabbard.

Up and up flowed the trail. The moon was directly overhead and the scene was almost as bright as day.

Abruptly the canyon widened and leveled off into a clearing where stood the remains of an ancient Indian village, to which the trail led.

And directly ahead, a fissure many feet in width and of unknown depth cut the canyon floor, slashing its walls on either side.

"Got him!" Slade exulted. "He'll have to pull up and we'll have the showdown!" He shoved the rifle to the front.

But Sosna did not pull up; he sent the chestnut charging forward. Slade exclaimed in horror: "He can't do it! No horse living can make that jump!"

Sosna did not draw rein. Slade saw him tense in the saddle, lean forward, plying the quirt with all his strength on the horse's heaving flanks.

"He can't do it!" Slade repeated.

The chestnut tried. With a scream of fear and protest, he launched himself into space. He screamed again, a high-pitched scream of terror and despair as he saw he'd jumped short.

Down he plunged! Veck Sosna turned in the saddle, waved derisively to his pursuer, and rode grandly into eternity!

Shaking, feeling more than a little sick, Slade pulled up on the lip of the cleft. In the still white flood of the moonlight he could just make out the motionless forms of horse and rider on the rocks sixty feet below.

"Guess he'll stay dead this time," he muttered and turned away from the grim gorge.

"I hope," he added morosely. For an instant he hesitated, his hand tightening on the bridle. Perhaps he should go back for another look into the canyon. But he was still shaken, still feeling sick. He dreaded to gaze again on that scene of horror. Oh, the devil! He was just being silly. Not even Veck Sosna could survive such a fall to the rocky floor of the gorge. Sosna was dead! He faced resolutely to the front and rode on.

For years Walt Slade had looked forward to the time when he and Veck Sosna should stand face to face in the final showdown and shoot it out. But now when all was over, he was glad that he hadn't killed Sosna. It would have been too much like a grudge killing.

A wave of sadness swept over him as he pondered that wasted life. In any legitimate enterprise, Veck Sosna could have reached the heights. Lucifer, Star of the Morning, with Heaven in the hollow of his hand, lowered his eyes to Hell!

When he reached the Fort Stockton Trail, Slade drew rein. To the south, he knew, another trail crossed it, a trail that led to the lower Comanche. With eyes that did not really see that upon which they rested, he gazed into the distance.

To the south were comfort, companionship, and, mayhap, peace. To the north—danger, new adventure, and duty.

He turned Shadow's nose to the north.

Center Point Large Print
600 Brooks Road / PO Box 1
Thorndike, ME 04986-0001 USA

(207) 568-3717

US & Canada:
1 800 929-9108
www.centerpointlargeprint.com